Critical Acclai

'A million readers can't ...
your day, sit back and ...
– How...

'Taut and compelling' – Peter James

'Leigh Russell is one to watch' – **Lee Child**

'A brilliant talent in the thriller field' – **Jeffery Deaver**

'Brilliant and chilling, Leigh Russell delivers a cracker of a read!' – **Martina Cole**

'Leigh Russell has become one of the most impressively dependable purveyors of the English police procedural' – *Times*

'DI Geraldine Steel is one of the most authoritative female coppers in a crowded field' – *Financial Times*

'The latest police procedural from prolific novelist Leigh Russell is as good and gripping as anything she has published' – *Times & Sunday Times Crime Club*

'Another corker of a book from Leigh Russell... Russell's talent for writing top-quality crime fiction just keeps on growing...' – *Euro Crime*

'Good, old-fashioned, heart-hammering police thriller... a no-frills delivery of pure excitement' – *SAGA Magazine*

'A gritty and totally addictive novel' – *New York Journal of Books*

Also by Leigh Russell

Poppy Mystery Tales
Barking Up the Right Tree
Barking Mad
Poppy Takes the Lead
Poppy's Christmas Cracker

Geraldine Steel Mysteries

Cut Short	*Deathly Affair*
Road Closed	*Deadly Revenge*
Dead End	*Evil Impulse*
Death Bed	*Deep Cover*
Stop Dead	*Guilt Edged*
Fatal Act	*Fake Alibi*
Killer Plan	*Final Term*
Murder Ring	*Without Trace*
Deadly Alibi	*Revenge Killing*
Class Murder	*Deadly Will*
Death Rope	*Cold Justice*
Rogue Killer	

Ian Peterson Murder Investigations
Cold Sacrifice
Race to Death
Blood Axe

Lucy Hall Mysteries
Journey to Death
Girl in Danger
The Wrong Suspect

The Adulterer's Wife
Suspicion

POPPY
plays
FAIR

———

LEIGH RUSSELL

A POPPY MYSTERY TALE

cmc

First published in 2025 by
The Crime & Mystery Club,
an imprint of Oldcastle Books Ltd.,
Harpenden, UK

crimeandmysteryclub.co.uk
@CrimeMystClub

ISBN
978-0-85730-602-9 (Paperback)
978-0-85730-603-6 (eBook)

2 4 6 8 10 9 7 5 3 1

Typeset in 12 on 14.35pt Monotype Sabon
by Avocet Typeset, Bideford, Devon, EX39 2BP

Printed and bound in Great Britain by
CPI Group (UK) Ltd, Croydon CR0 4YY

MIX
Paper | Supporting
responsible forestry
FSC® C013604

The manufacturer's authorised representative in the EU for product safety is Easy Access System Europe, Mustamäe tee 50, 10621 Tallinn, Estonia
gpsr.requests@easproject.com

This story is dedicated to Lily, who sadly passed away before the book was published. Enjoy the unlimited treats in doggy heaven and rest in peace, beloved little Lily.

1

EVERY YEAR THE RESIDENTS of Ashton Mead anticipated the annual summer fair with varying degrees of excitement and trepidation. Working as a waitress in the local tea shop, I overheard customers expressing their views. Some of the locals deplored any disturbance to the peaceful life of the village and grumbled to one another about strangers running rampant through the streets.

'We don't want hordes of showpeople roaming around our village.'

'It's not the showpeople, it's all the visitors who drop litter everywhere.'

'I blame the council. They don't put enough bins out. I mean, how difficult can it be?'

'… and the noise.'

'Remember last year? Old Meg Forster's grandson was mugged in broad daylight.'

Others were excited at the prospect of the fair returning to the grassy slopes near the river and talked enthusiastically about taking their grandchildren on rides.

'This year I promised to take him on the big wheel.'

'… the bumper cars.'

'… the merry-go-round.'

'… the helter-skelter.'

My best friend and boss, Hannah, was cautiously pleased about the fair, which always attracted visitors from neighbouring villages, and even from the nearest town of Swindon. More people coming to the village translated into more customers for the tea shop. Hannah fretted about her tea shop which, so far, was thriving, thanks to her hard work and scrumptious baking. She insisted that a business needed to grow if it was to survive. It was true that current success was no guarantee of future prosperity and her profits were precarious, so she was understandably worried about the future. Owning a café had always been her dream, and when she had received a generous divorce settlement from her ex-husband, she had invested the lot in the Sunshine Tea Shoppe. When I had moved into the picturesque cottage left to me by my great aunt, Hannah had offered me a job. Without that modest income, I might not have been able to stay, and I had fallen in love with my property and with the lovely village.

In the three years that I had been working for Hannah, my mother had not hidden her snobbish disdain for my job, but I was very happy working as a waitress. Not only was I spending every day with my best friend, but I could walk to work. When Hannah's mother was unable to look after my little dog, Poppy could stay in the yard at the back of the café. When it rained, she slept in her little bed in a corner of the kitchen. Poppy had been bequeathed to me by my great aunt, along with her cottage, Rosecroft. Never having owned a dog before, I had been nervous to begin with, but Poppy was irresistible. A Jack Tzu, with white and brown fur and an expressive face, she was not only adorable, but highly intelligent. Living alone, I very quickly came to rely on her companionship. Unlike any boyfriend I had ever had, Poppy never let me down, not even for an instant. I could no longer imagine life without her.

Following a dry spell, the morning before the fair was due to arrive in Ashton Mead there was a torrential downpour, but the weather cleared up by early evening. Poppy and I wandered down to the grassy slopes by the river to watch the fair being set up. Poppy trotted around happily sniffing the ground at every step, while I trod carefully to avoid the worst of the mud. Even so, from time to time my boots squelched as I walked, and I resigned myself to the fact that they would need to be cleaned after our walk. It was impossible not to marvel at the speed and deftness with which the stalls and rides were being erected. Within a few hours, the scene would undergo a complete transformation from an empty open space to a bustling hub of fairground attractions. Indistinct figures strode in and out of shadows cast by bright lights illuminating a strange scene, men and women dragging poles, trestle tables, curious chunks of brightly coloured plastic, coiled wires and bags of tacky prizes. Underlying the seemingly haphazard activity, there was a sense of purpose in the hectic scene.

Hearing raised voices, I peered around and was surprised to make out the familiar form of Dana Flack. A newcomer to Ashton Mead, she had come to live on the outskirts of the village when she lost her job as a reporter on the local paper. While she had been working as a journalist, I had found her arrogant and intrusive, and had done my best to avoid her. Since she had been made redundant, she had taken to hanging around the village looking so crestfallen that I almost felt sorry for her. This evening, she appeared to be arguing with a blonde woman whose shrill voice penetrated the general din of clattering metal and shouted instructions.

'You're just jealous, that's what it is,' I heard the blonde woman snap as Poppy and I came within earshot.

Poppy growled very softly, almost furtively, as though she understood we might not want to be caught eavesdropping.

'You think I'm jealous?' Dana scoffed, tossing her head and flicking her black hair off her sharp-featured face. 'You can't be serious, not after everything he's done. And you know as well as I do that it's all true.'

After that, Dana said something about it being the best decision she ever made, and the other woman laughed with obvious derision.

'What the hell are you doing here, anyway?' the blonde woman demanded. 'You don't belong here with us, and you're not welcome here neither.'

'I've got as much right to be here as anyone else,' Dana replied. Her words were defiant, but she sounded tired and in the semi-darkness I could see that her shoulders were bowed in defeat. 'You can't dictate where I can and can't go. It's a free country.'

'Free!' the other woman echoed scornfully. 'You can't stand there and tell me you're free of him.'

The woman took a step towards Dana so that they were almost touching. Her hair was unkempt and she looked younger than Dana, who must have been in her thirties. The stranger's arms were hanging down at her sides but, as she moved into a patch of dusky light, I could see her fists were clenched. 'Why have you come here?' the blonde woman repeated. This time, she no longer sounded hostile, but genuinely curious.

Poppy whimpered. Scooping her up in my arms, I scurried away before the two women noticed us watching. We passed several other shadowy figures who were busily setting up stalls and rides. Voices rang out all around us in the gathering darkness.

'Easy there.'

'I've got it.'

'You're too far over.'

'Nearly done.'

The preparations went on far into the night, long after Poppy and I had gone home and been lulled to sleep by the distant clatter and shouts coming from the direction of the river.

The rain did not return and, on my way to work the next morning, I took a short detour through the fair. Most of the setting up had been completed the previous night. Although the stalls around the perimeter were not yet manned, and the food vans were still closed, we could hear distant thumping music coming from the merry-go-round. The roar and rattle of rides grew louder as we approached the centre of the site, where a generator contributed a background drone to the blaring noise of the attractions. Walking around the outer circle we passed a shooting gallery where a few boys were hanging around, waiting to try their luck. As we walked on, the stall holder began to take their money. The sharp popping sounds of the guns made Poppy shiver nervously so I picked her up and held her close as I walked on, passing yellow ducks bobbing up and down, impossible to hook, a mirror maze and a ghost train, a coconut shy and a sweet smelling candy floss stall. Assailed by so many new smells, Poppy fussed to be put down. She trotted along beside me, constantly alert, her eyes darting around, her nose raised to explore a conglomeration of smells carried on the air: oil and axle grease mingled with the cloying scent of sugar.

'This is all very interesting, isn't it?' I asked her.

She glanced up at me briefly before turning her attention back to her surroundings, as if to tell me she was very busy sniffing all the different scents that had arrived on the grass by the river, and had no time to listen to me. We walked on, both of us enjoying the sights and smells and nascent exuberance of the fair. By late morning, the area would be packed with people, but we couldn't stay around to watch the crowds arrive. It was time to head to the tea shop to serve breakfast. Hoping my long red hair wouldn't smell of the fairground, I hurried to work. We had a busy morning and there was no chance for Hannah and I to chat, but I overheard quite a few customers talking about the fair in the village. Some people were pleased about it, particularly those who had children or grandchildren. Others were less enthusiastic. After grumbling about the prices of the rides, the conversation moved on.

'That's hardly fair,' one woman piped up, hearing someone complain about the litter the fair would inevitably leave behind. 'It's visitors – members of the public – who leave a load of rubbish behind when they go home, and the fairground workers are expected to clear up.'

'It's the youngsters,' someone else said. 'No respect for the environment.'

That prompted another discussion, with some customers criticising teenagers, while others defended them vigorously. Listening from the kitchen, Hannah smiled. Pleased that the tea shop had become a popular social hub for many retired customers, she felt she was providing a valuable service to people who might otherwise feel isolated.

'And it doesn't hurt your profits to have a nucleus of regular customers,' I added.

'That's a very cynical way of looking at it,' she told me with a disapproving scowl.

'Whatever you say,' I grinned. We both knew I was right.

After lunch, I took a short break to give Poppy a walk, and to look around the fair again. During the day, the fair was mainly packed with families eager to enjoy a day out: children begging and cajoling and becoming hyperactive, having scoffed more sugar than was good for them; grandparents indulging their young charges; and parents trying to curb the spending spree. Most of the rides were noticeably more expensive than the previous year. In common with everything else, prices were going up, which added to Hannah's worries. Increased running costs were affecting profits in the tea shop, where Hannah was doing her best to avoid having to put her prices up. Fortunately, few customers seemed to notice the subtle tactics she adopted to save money. Reducing the thickness of a scone by twenty per cent passed unnoticed, whereas an increase of a few pence on a cup of tea caused comments and raised eyebrows.

'You can't stand still in business,' she complained. 'If you're not moving forward you're going backwards.'

But where once Hannah had been optimistically making plans to extend the café or even purchase a second premises, in the current economic climate she was now having to work hard to maintain her current situation.

I pressed on, walking through the fair, dodging baby strollers and loiterers, and negotiating a path through the growing crowds, until I reached the innermost rides: the helter-skelter, the jangling carousel, the big wheel and the dodgems. Here the noise was almost deafening, loud music overlaid with intermittent waves of screaming coming from the rides, along with people yelling to be heard above the general din, a cacophony that drowned out the hum of the generator. Later on, in the evening, teenagers would gather in gangs and the atmosphere would become more menacing as darkness approached. But during the day, the fair was a fun place to while away an idle half hour on my break.

Even in the daytime atmosphere of good cheer, it was still a little risky walking around. Tugging at his mother's hand and not looking where he was going, a small boy collided with me and began bawling.

His mother instantly turned on me with a ferocious frown. 'Here, watch where you're going.'

Sensing a threat, Poppy barked. Before I had a chance to remonstrate that the child had barged into me, the woman scooped her little boy up in her arms and elbowed her way off through the crowd. If it hadn't been for Poppy yapping aggressively at her, she might not have been so ready to walk away. Even though she had deprived me of an opportunity to explain what had happened, I was pleased to see her go. I suspected any attempt to remonstrate would have ended in an angry confrontation. We sauntered on without further incident, mainly following the crowd, and manoeuvring our way around people going in the opposite direction, greeting neighbours and regular customers of the tea shop as we made our way slowly past the different rides. Seeing my next-door neighbour, Richard, who owned the only other house in Mill Lane, I paused for a brief chat, but the noise made communication almost impossible and we soon abandoned any attempt at conversation, instead settling for smiles and thumbs up gestures. I saw the tall figure of Dana Flack striding along. She was glancing around uneasily as though searching for someone, or perhaps avoiding them, and hanging around like a lost soul.

'That woman needs to get a job,' Hannah had told me one afternoon when Dana sat lingering in the tea shop over a solitary cup of tea.

'Well, she's not having mine,' I said.

'As if I could manage without you,' Hannah replied, and I grinned.

In the centre of the fairground, the noise, the movement of people, and the different colours and flashing lights of the rides became overwhelming after a short time. Even Poppy seemed less alert. Her eyes began to close as she flagged under the assault of unfamiliar smells and loud noises. We walked on past bellowing barkers, their voices ringing out above the hubbub.

'Three throws for a fiver!'

'Roll up! Roll up!'

'Step right this way, ladies and gentlemen, for the big wheel!'

'A prize every time!'

'The scariest experience of your life!'

'Everyone's a winner!'

'How about it, darling?' a man called out to me as I paused by his stall to pick Poppy up. He dangled a small plastic bag with a little goldfish in it. 'Three throws for a tenner, and a one in three guarantee of success.' He grinned as he offered me the chance to hand over ten pounds for nothing. 'I can see you're an animal lover,' he added cheerily, nodding at Poppy who was snuggling comfortably in my arms. 'He's a real beauty. What do you call him?'

Poppy growled and watched him warily. A stray strand of candy floss floated past and she snapped at it, momentarily distracted. Shaking my head at the barker, and laughing at his glib patter, I continued on my way. After a while I came across my friend Barry, the local policeman. He was on duty in his uniform, and we walked on together for a few minutes. We reached the centre of the fairground, where the big rides rang out their strident tunes. A man leaped nimbly off a pole on the carousel and held out a calloused hand.

'Fancy a ride, darling?' he shouted, winking suggestively at me.

Under other circumstances I might have been tempted to take his hand, he was so attractive. But Poppy growled and I shook my head, smiling into his dark eyes. I had learned to trust Poppy's instincts, and her hostility warned me to be wary. Experience had taught me that good looks were no indication of reliable character in a man. Besides, I didn't think Poppy would be comfortable riding on the carousel in my arms. A woman appeared behind him on the running board of the carousel and I was almost sure she was the woman I had seen arguing with Dana on the previous evening when the fair was being set up. Blonde and pretty, under the bright lights of the ride she looked as though she was barely out of her teens. Her make-up failed to conceal a black eye, and when one of her sleeves slipped back, she pulled it down quickly, but not before I had spotted a bruise on her wrist. Knocks and accidents were probably common enough in such a physically demanding environment, but it crossed my mind to wonder whether someone had been beating her up. Her eyes met mine for an instant, her expression defiant yet frightened.

'Alfie,' she addressed her good-looking colleague. 'Marge wants you to turn her music up. The volume button's stuck.'

'Tell her to fix it herself,' he muttered. 'I got my own ride to run.'

I shook my head and, with a breezy grin, he was gone, searching for his next punter.

I walked on with Poppy in my arms, resisting the ghost train and the dodgems. Poppy gazed longingly whenever a child passed us brandishing a stick of pink and white spun candy floss, and when we approached a food stall, she became frantic to jump down. I knew it was wrong to spoil her, but I stopped and bought a hot dog and shared the sausage with her, telling myself she was entitled to enjoy all the fun of the fair along with everyone else. We had almost completed half a circuit of the site, and I was about to turn back towards the tea shop, when a piercing scream penetrated the ambient clamour. The big wheel abruptly stopped turning. A fairground worker standing on the back of a bumper car shouted a command, and the cars slid to a halt. A message seemed to be telepathically relayed right across the main site because, as if by magic, all the music ceased. Only one jingly tune continued for a moment after the others had stopped. It rang out for a few seconds, thin and haunting, and then it too fell silent.

People around me stopped shoving and bustling. Those queueing for rides turned to look for the source of the scream. Men in greasy jeans began racing from ride to ride, leaping over couplings and wires encased in thick rubber tubes. Other showmen left their stalls or jumped down from runner boards to join them. Before long, at least a dozen fairground workers were charging towards the big wheel. An eerie hush descended on the central area of the fairground. The constant hum of the generator became audible once more. Visitors to the fair huddled in groups, murmuring and whispering as rumours started circulating around the crowd. A man had plummeted from the big wheel; a boy had leaned too far over the edge of the helter-skelter and had fallen to his death; a woman had been flung from the carousel and died after landing on her head and breaking her neck. Any one of those speculations could be true, but most people standing near me thought it was more likely to be a power outage.

'It can't be the power because the generator's still working,' I pointed out to a woman standing next to me.

She nodded. We could hear the uninterrupted droning of the generator.

'It could be a problem with the internal connections,' she suggested.

Her companion laughed at her. 'Stop trying to sound as though you know what you're talking about,' he said. 'You're not an electrician.'

'What's your explanation for the rides all stopping then, if you're so clever?' she asked him.

Before he could reply, the crowd parted to allow a pair of first aiders to hurry towards the big wheel, closely followed by a couple of uniformed police officers. I recognised one of them as my friend, Barry. I stared at him in consternation as we heard the wailing of approaching sirens. A moment later, the arrival of paramedics seemed to confirm that someone had met with an accident. Their presence suggested it was serious.

The crowd surged forwards in the wake of the police. Barry and his colleague did their best to hold onlookers back. As far as we could tell, someone had been injured between the helter-skelter and the Ferris wheel, making it relatively easy for two police officers to block onlookers from coming too close to the body. It was impossible to see if the casualty was alive, but the fact that the paramedics appeared to be busy meant that the victim might have survived. No one around us seemed to know what had happened, although a rumour was spreading that someone had witnessed a body plummeting from one of the rides. It wasn't long before a team of police officers arrived to set up a complete cordon around the scene of the accident. Some onlookers, particularly those with children, began to drift away. With nothing further to see, the youngsters soon tired of waiting.

Hannah arrived, wanting to find out if there was any truth in the news that had by now reached the tea shop. She could only stay for a minute. 'We could be waiting here for hours,' she said. 'You can stay and see what happens, if you like. I have to run straight back, but don't feel you have to come with me.' She had phoned her boyfriend, Adam, to tell him that there had been an accident at the fair, and he joined us.

Even though I wanted to stay and find out what had happened, I agreed to accompany her. After all, it was my job to wait on tables in the tea shop, while Hannah prepared the orders. The brief lull between lunch and tea was over. We decided to leave Adam waiting by the police cordon. Hannah made him promise to report back to us as soon as he had discovered what had happened. She exhorted him to pump Barry for information if the cause of the drama was concealed from the waiting crowd, as seemed likely.

'Remember, ask Barry,' Hannah reminded as we were leaving. 'Tell him Emily wants to know.' She grinned at me and winked at Adam.

I frowned at her. It was no secret that Barry fancied me, and she was evidently hoping it might be possible to cajole him into revealing confidential information to curry favour with me.

Meanwhile, we had to hurry to prepare for a rush of tea-time customers, and so we made our way back through the crowd as quickly we could.

'Let's hope Adam gets here soon with details about the accident,' Hannah said, as we were preparing the first tea trays. 'I don't want to sound ghoulish, but I really want to know what all the fuss is about.'

I nodded. Life in the village was often eventful, but an incident as dramatic as someone plunging from a fairground attraction was unusual, and I shared my friend's curiosity.

'It's not ghoulish,' I assured her. 'It's natural to want to find out what happened.'

Before long, we were too busy to chat, but the disturbance at the fair was impossible to forget. Everyone was talking about it in the tea shop.

2

AS WE HAD ANTICIPATED, the tea shop was very busy that Saturday and we spent most of the afternoon running around serving customers. Although the pressure was stressful, it was also gratifying in the light of Hannah's concerns over the precarious position of her business. Only one couple sat for an hour sharing a single pot of tea. People like that exasperated me, because their table could have accommodated customers willing to spend more money. Where I was irritated, Hannah was tolerant.

'Perhaps that's all they can afford,' she would say.

After a while I stopped grumbling to her, because it only prompted her to give away free buns and scones to customers who ordered next to nothing but sat eking out a single pot of tea. With the recent sharp rise in the cost of living, their number increased for a while. Hard-pressed to keep up with orders, Hannah usually wasn't aware of their presence unless I drew attention to them. Somehow she seemed unwilling to accept the connection between her bouts of liberality and her fluctuating profits. In a way she was right, because she insisted she only made a gift of surplus scones that were likely to be thrown away anyway. My concern was that her generosity attracted people who didn't want to spend much, and they were not the regular customers we wanted to encourage. It galled me whenever we had to turn paying customers away, while a table was occupied by hangers-on who were literally eating into our profits. In the uncertain economic climate, it seemed important to guard against gaining a reputation for giving away free food.

Hannah was obdurate and, since she was the boss, I had to ostensibly support her views. To be fair, there are worse criticisms to level against someone than to accuse them of being generous. Nevertheless, I quietly did my best to ensure she didn't know when any familiar freeloaders arrived, so she wouldn't automatically start giving away food. At times we had seemed dangerously close to donating more food than we sold. Gradually, thanks mainly to my vigilance, the scroungers stopped swamping us before the business foundered. Hannah was pleased that her profits had improved, and I kept silent about my covert mission to save the tea shop from financial ruin. I tried to convince myself that I was acting selflessly to support my friend, but I was protecting my own livelihood as well.

Since losing her job, former journalist Dana Flack had become a regular customer at the tea shop. While she had been working for the local paper, I had mistrusted her. Turning up whenever anyone was in trouble, she would scavenge through people's misery for a newsworthy scandal, like a literate vulture. Now she was no longer poking her nose into other people's affairs, she turned out to be unexpectedly good company. Two single women who had both arrived in Ashton Mead as adults, it was natural for us to strike up a friendship. We sometimes chatted in the tea shop while Hannah was busy in the kitchen, and occasionally arranged to meet for a pint in The Plough.

'How long were you living here before your neighbours stopped treating you like you had dropped in from another planet?' she had asked me one evening when we were having a drink together in the pub.

I had laughed. 'I've been living here for over three years and many of the locals still regard me as a newcomer.'

'An alien, more like,' she had muttered to her pint.

I had nodded. My answer hadn't given the whole picture. While some villagers persisted in treating me as an outsider, many had welcomed me into the life of the village fairly quickly. It helped that my great aunt had lived there for years, long enough for her to be accepted as a bona fide member of the village community, many of whom couldn't remember a time before she had settled there. My relationship with my great aunt was one reason why the locals accepted me so readily. In addition to my family connection, there was my property, which I was careful to maintain. I also had a job in the village and was good friends with Hannah, Toby and Barry, all of whom had been born and raised in Ashton Mead. My one neighbour in Mill Lane had moved to the village sometime after me, and his arrival had also helped to make me feel relatively settled there. Keen to establish a rapport with Dana, I realised that not having lived in Ashton Mead all our lives gave us something in common. So I had played down how quickly I had been accepted by the local community, instead making out that I too felt as though I was treated more or less like a stranger. Over a companionable pint, we had agreed that it was mainly the older inhabitants of the village who insisted on regarding us as outsiders.

'I hadn't realised how insular people here are,' she had admitted plaintively. 'I was sick of the pressures of urban living, and thought somewhere more rural would make a nice change. But people here aren't exactly hospitable. I mean they're very pleasant, and everyone's civil, but almost everyone I meet seems to have lived here all their life, and everyone knows everyone else. In a way it's worse than the anonymity of living in town because I don't know anything about anyone else, but everyone seems to know all about me. I feel as though I have no privacy.'

As though sympathising with Dana's despondency, Poppy had gone over to her and nuzzled her feet. Dana had reached down to pet her and Poppy had rolled over onto her back, pleased at the attention.

'You'll get used to it,' I had assured my new friend. 'And you'll get to know the locals eventually. You just need to be patient. Give it another fifty years and they'll be making you feel right at home here.'

We both laughed.

'I'm used to being a pariah,' she had admitted, taking a gulp of her beer.

'What do you mean?'

Dana had looked at me but hadn't answered my question directly. 'I used to have to cover the fair for the paper,' she said. 'It's going to be strange seeing it just as a member of the public, not as a reporter. I keep feeling a compulsion to take notes whenever something happens.' She shrugged. 'Of course, I had to report on it from the viewpoint of an uninterested outsider, and that in itself was pretty weird for me. But the editor sent me there, and it was more than my job was worth to refuse a commission. Not that all that kowtowing got me anywhere. I still ended up on the scrapheap. No one values hard work and dedication, not in the media industry anyway.' She stared morosely at her glass.

Listening to her, I had been puzzled. 'Aren't we all "outsiders" at the fair?' I had asked her.

'Oh, I thought you knew. I grew up on the fairground.' She had given a hollow laugh. Seeing my surprised expression, she had continued. 'So I'm used to feeling like an outsider, never fully accepted by society. And now my own people have turned their backs on me.'

'Why would they do that?'

'You can't understand how it works if you haven't experienced it. Living on a travelling fair is not like any other way of life. We're always on the move, for a start, and it's hard work. There's no let up.' She had paused to take another swig of beer. 'It's a close-knit group and, as long as you're one of them, they protect you fiercely. To the death, if need be. Literally. But once you leave them, you're an outcast. Family loyalty means everything to fairground people and, if you leave, you're regarded as a traitor to the community.'

'With mainstream society suspicious of them, I suppose they have to stick together,' I had murmured.

'Yes, but it goes deeper than that. It's hard to explain our traditions to someone who hasn't lived with them. Whatever you do, you're supported. Honour among thieves and all that.' She had smiled, before continuing gravely. 'Even the most heinous crimes are forgiven, as long as they're kept hidden from the outside world. Don't get me wrong, most travelling showpeople are simple good-hearted purveyors of entertainment. We're not bad people. At least, we're no worse than anyone else, and a lot less judgemental than some. But the point is, my people stick together. We have to, for our own protection. Travelling showpeople are spread all over the country and have a web of communication that would put any spy network to shame. Now that I've left, I'm treated with suspicion by showpeople all over the world,' she concluded.

'Who do they need protecting from?' I had asked uneasily, although I knew the answer.

'Oh, everyone,' was the vague reply. 'People, society. Everyone likes the fun of the fair, but no one likes the people who turn up and provide the entertainment. It's a constant struggle to keep going. My father was the boss of our crew, which meant it was his job to negotiate with the authorities for permission to trade, and those licences are precarious. They can be revoked at the first sign of trouble. Even as a child, I was aware of the hurdles he had to overcome just to keep the fair going. He took care of the showpeople, and he had years of experience in dealing with all the bureaucracy. He was a good boss.' She sighed. 'There were lean times for the fair after my father was killed.'

'Did you say he was killed?' I had asked her, startled by what she was telling me.

Dana had shrugged, her dark eyes troubled. 'The community picked themselves up again, but I'd left the fair by then. I couldn't bear to stay on after what happened to my father. I think some of them blamed me for what happened. At any rate, they don't trust me. They can only suspect what I know, and that makes them uneasy. They're still watching me.'

The conversation had taken a sinister turn, and I hadn't been sure what to make of it. I had really warmed to Dana, and had been keen to express my sympathy for her situation, but I was floundering. None of the usual platitudes had seemed appropriate, given what she was telling me. As though sensing my quandary, Poppy had nuzzled Dana's feet and my friend had leaned down to pet her. After that interruption, I had been relieved when Dana had started talking about the tea shop, and we had chatted about other matters for another half hour before going home. Dana had been interested to hear about my last long term boyfriend, who had dumped me only to reappear when he heard about my inheritance.

'I was a mug to fall for his lies,' I admitted. 'He was a charmer, but he lied shamelessly. He hated Ashton Mead and was desperate for me to sell Rosecroft, but what really opened my eyes to his true character was when he tried to sell Poppy behind my back. She had never liked him.'

'I'm not surprised. He sounds like a real louse. You're better off without him.'

I nodded.

'So,' she went on, smiling, 'is there anyone else?'

Sheepishly I admitted that the local policeman, Barry, had kissed me at Christmas.

'It was a silly thing,' I said. 'Under the mistletoe, you know, and we were both a bit tipsy. But it's no secret that he wants to go out with me. We did actually have a date once, but it never came to anything. The thing is, he's a decent guy and I like him a lot, but I'm not sure I fancy him. That is, I wasn't until he kissed me.' I paused, embarrassed at having confessed my feelings. 'You're the only person I've admitted that to. Usually I talk about everything with Hannah, but I can't talk about Barry with her because she's friends with him, which makes it awkward. Whatever you do, promise me you won't say a word about this to her. They grew up in the village and went to the same school and she's very fond of him. She knows he likes me, and she's always on at me to go out with him.'

Dana gave me her word she would be discreet, and I trusted her. It was a relief to be able to talk to someone about my feelings for Barry.

'I'm glad you've come to live in the village,' I told her, and she beamed.

The following day I had mentioned Dana's problems to Hannah, who had laughingly dismissed my concern.

'It sounds to me as though she was trying to make herself appear more interesting than she really is. I dare say she can't help it. I mean, when she was working on the newspaper, it was her job to spy out potential drama, and exaggerate whatever stories she came across to make them sound really sensational. It may well be true that she grew up on a fairground, but if you ask me, that's interesting enough without any added drama about murders and being watched. The part about the fairground community not liking it when she left them is plausible, I suppose, but the rest of it sounds to me like paranoid rambling. As for her father being some kind of organised crime boss, surely that has to be a gross exaggeration.'

'She never said anything about an organised crime gang,' I had protested, half laughing. 'Now who's being melodramatic?'

Whatever the truth was, we had agreed it must have been hard for Dana to be cast out by her community, and

28

snubbed by everyone she knew. Being dismissed from her job on the paper must have damaged her self-confidence even further.

'Poor Dana. We have to do our best to be kind to her,' Hannah had said.

I had nodded, silently hoping that didn't mean Hannah would start showering Dana with free food.

'It might be best if we don't tell anyone else about Dana growing up with the fairground people,' she had added. 'It shouldn't make any difference, but it probably wouldn't help her to be accepted here. People can be very narrow-minded, especially if they've only ever lived here in the village. I dread to think what stories Maud would come up with if she learned about Dana's past.'

Later in the afternoon on the day of the fair, Hannah and I were both rushed off our feet. We could have done with Adam to help us, but we had left him at the fair with strict instructions not to join us until he was able to bring us news about the accident. Meanwhile, at every table customers were earnestly discussing what had happened.

'It was a fatal accident, if ever there was one,' a woman in a red sun hat announced to two other women at her table. 'Probably murder,' she added darkly, glancing around the room to see who else was listening to her.

'You can't possibly know that,' one of her companions replied. 'Anything could have happened. That's just speculation.'

'Idle speculation,' someone at a neighbouring table chipped in. 'You shouldn't go spreading rumours like that.'

'Was I talking to you?' the woman in the red hat looked round and retorted stoutly, before turning back to her companions. 'Why else would police be there?' she continued, raising her voice so the customers at the next table could hear her. 'And why were they so keen to keep people away? There was something going on all right and I, for one, intend to find out exactly what it was.'

'How are you going to do that?' one of her companions asked, leaning forward eagerly.

'I don't know yet, but we have a right to know what's going on in our own village.'

The arrival of Maud, the owner of the village store, caused a stir; well known as a gossip, she had a reputation for knowing everything that went on in the village. Her interest in local affairs was not mere curiosity. Many of her customers only shopped at the village store so they could keep up with the latest tittle-tattle about their neighbours. If anyone knew what had happened earlier in the fair she would, although, since her recent marriage to the local butcher, her information was no longer always new.

'What have you heard, Maud?' an elderly man called out to her across the room, and a hush descended over the other customers as we all waited to hear her reply. Everyone turned to look at Maud, who gazed around the room, her beady eyes glinting with satisfaction at the attention she was attracting. 'Well,' she said slowly, settling into a chair and clasping her capacious pink handbag on her lap, 'the presence of the police means they suspect foul play.' Her hair, worn in a blonde perm since her wedding, twitched as she nodded her head complacently.

'We realise that,' the woman in the red sun hat said impatiently.

'On the contrary, we can't know that for sure,' the old man interjected.

'You asked me, and that's what I think,' Maud replied, clearly nettled.

'I'm not saying you're wrong. You could be right,' the old man conceded. 'All I'm saying is it's not necessarily the case. They could be investigating a serious accident.'

Looking irritated, Maud began studying the menu. A few people started muttering about rides being unsafe, and steps being taken to punish those responsible.

'They'll close that fair down,' the woman in the red sun hat announced firmly. 'You wait and see. They can't let them walk away from this unscathed, as though nothing happened. Whoever's responsible for their safety measures ought to be charged with criminal negligence.'

The woman in the sun hat's remark prompted a chorus of comments.

'The person in charge should be locked up,' someone added.

'The whole site needs to be closed.'

'They should never be allowed to set up that fair again.'

'Serves them right if they close it down.'

'Health and safety regulations would ride a coach and horses through that fair.'

'The owners should be sued,' a woman said.

Across the room, Dana looked up from a seat in the corner and her eyes met mine. I recalled her saying how difficult it was to obtain licences to operate in the first place, and how precarious they were once they had been acquired. She shrugged, as if to say: 'You see, everyone enjoys the fair, but no one likes the people who work there.'

'It could have been a child that fell to its death,' someone else added.

A brief argument broke out over whether the death of a child would be a worse tragedy than an adult falling to their death. Either way someone would have died. Disappointingly, Maud actually had very little news to share beyond what we all already knew. The police remained guarded in what they were prepared to divulge at this stage. If someone *had* died, in tragic circumstances, the victim's family would need to be notified before any information was made public. Maud was seated with a couple of her cronies and she began murmuring to them, and other customers resumed their previous conversations.

Once the initial rush was over, there was a slight lull before closing time, and I noticed Dana had not moved from her table in the corner of the room. Her face was drawn, and her eyes looked around dully, as though she was struggling to register what she was seeing. Usually alert to everything that was going on around her, she barely glanced up at my approach. It was time for me to take a five minute break, so I sat down with her over a pot of tea and a plate of scones, intending to quiz her about what had happened earlier at the fair. As a former member of the fairground community, I wondered if she would be able to shed any new light on the incident. When I started to question her, she frowned and lowered her voice before answering.

'What happened today, at the fair, it was—' she hesitated and glanced around before adding, 'I don't think what happened today was an accident.' She paused before murmuring under her breath, 'I think it was murder, and I think it was meant for me.'

3

THE FOLLOWING DAY WE had a quiet patch in the middle of the morning, and Hannah sent me out to buy a few items from the village shop. More often than not, I left Poppy with Hannah's mother during the day. After a slightly unpropitious start, Poppy and Jane's old dog, Holly, had settled down comfortably in one another's company. Today, Jane was meeting a friend in Swindon, and Poppy was spending the day with us at the tea shop, so I was pleased to have an opportunity to take her for a walk. As long as the weather was dry, it was a leisurely stroll to the village store when Poppy was with me, as she insisted on stopping every few feet to sniff the grass and add her frequent messages for other dogs who passed by. On such a lovely day, I was happy to take my time and enjoy the sunshine before returning to the sometimes frenetic activity in the tea shop. Even with the kitchen door open at the back it could become quite stuffy inside the tea shop, especially when it was full, and it was a relief to step outside into the fresh air. I shook my head, appreciating the cool breeze blowing through my hair.

'It's all right for you,' I told Poppy. 'All you have to do at the tea shop is laze in the yard, watching for birds flying past, or curl up in your basket in the nice warm kitchen and go to sleep. I have to be on my feet all day, waiting at tables.'

Poppy let out a quiet growl, as if to say, 'And that's just as it should be, after all my hard work patrolling the garden for foxes.'

Well behaved dogs were allowed in the village shop as long as they were carried. As soon as I entered with Poppy in my arms, Maud beckoned me over.

'Have you heard?' she murmured, without even pausing to greet me.

Her eyes were alight with glee, and her nose almost seemed to be twitching in her eagerness to share her news. She resembled a grinning little mouse.

'What do you mean? Heard what?'

'They've arrested Dana Flack,' Maud announced with an air of triumph, as though she was personally responsible for having prevented a major catastrophe.

This was certainly dramatic, and the kind of news Maud loved to share. Local residents would visit the shop, ostensibly to make a purchase, but really to hear what she had to tell them. And, of course, while they were in the shop, they would feel obliged to buy something. In some ways it could be regarded as a very effective business model, only it was based on scandalmongering of which I disapproved, especially since I had fallen foul of Maud's canards myself. Many people had, which made it strange that so many of us still paid attention to her. Perhaps it was a kind of wilful blindness; few people wholly trusted what Maud said, yet we all listened avidly to her sensational tales. Maud seemed to absorb tittle-tattle from the ether. It seemed impossible for one person to know so much about what went on in the village, yet Maud's tales often turned out to be true, however far-fetched they sounded.

All at once, Maud's expression grew serious. 'Don't tell anyone,' she said with an air of urgency. 'We need to keep it to ourselves. I only mentioned it to you because I know you're friends with her. She wouldn't want everyone to know. She'll probably be home soon, and no one else will ever need to hear about it.'

She was probably afraid I would spread her news to customers in the tea shop, and deprive her of the opportunity to share the rumour herself.

'But are you sure they arrested her?' I asked.

While Maud was sometimes vague in her insinuations, on this occasion she sounded certain. She nodded, her bright eyes fixed on mine, as though to fix my attention on her.

'Wendy White lives over the road to Dana, and she saw it all,' she said.

It was my turn to nod. Wendy was one of Maud's cronies. In her nineties, she was sprightly enough to make her way to the village shop to listen to Maud's gossip. In some ways, Maud performed a valuable social service conveying local news to several elderly villagers who lived alone and would otherwise have nothing interesting going on in their lives. Yet behind the rumours and petty scandals that she shared lay real stories involving human misery. Maud was not a cruel woman, but she was shallow and thoughtless. She never seemed to reflect on what might lie behind the rumours she spread, or to consider who might be hurt by her news. All she was concerned about was to have some interesting snippet to share. I was inclined to forgive her, despite the potentially harmful consequences of her allegations, as I understood she used her gossip to attract custom.

'A marked police car drew up outside Dana's house about an hour ago,' Maud went on, becoming increasingly animated as she warmed to her tale. 'Two police officers got out. They were both in uniform, mind, so Wendy was in no doubt about who they were. She was desperate for a pee but she didn't dare abandon her post at her window, in case something happened while she was away. It's just as well she stayed, or she would have missed it.'

Feeling uneasy, I urged her to carry on with her account. 'Missed what? What happened?'

'Dana was frogmarched out of her own front door and driven away in the police car. Wendy saw it with her own eyes. They must have taken her to the police station in Swindon.' She shook her head, her jubilant expression at odds with her next words. 'Such a pity. Poor Dana. I wonder what she's done. She never was one of us, of course,' she added in a comment both callous and irrelevant.

'She probably hasn't done anything wrong, and you're jumping to the worst possible conclusion,' I pointed out frostily. Dana was, after all, my friend. 'The police could be questioning her as a witness. I don't think you should be casting aspersions on her character when you don't know what's going on.'

Reluctant to start an argument, I refrained from voicing my disgust at her blatant prejudice against a newcomer to the village. Quite a few of us had moved to the village as adults and we weren't criminals, and it wasn't as if every villager was innocent of wrongdoing. Maud's bias was completely groundless.

Maud nodded thoughtfully. 'Well, you know Dana, don't you? What's your opinion of her? Do you think she has criminal tendencies?'

'Of course not,' I burst out, exasperated that she would even ask that question. 'She's no more a criminal than you or me.'

'You sound pretty sure.'

'That's because I am. And I'm also sure that if I don't get back to the tea shop soon, Hannah's going to be really annoyed with me.'

After making my few purchases, I left the shop. Poppy trotted contentedly beside me, pausing frequently to sniff the ground, but I scarcely noticed her. As far as she was concerned, my sole reason for walking to the shop and back was for her to check the latest scents left by other dogs or even the occasional fox wandering nonchalantly along the village streets. But while she happily pursued her own agenda, my thoughts were in a whirl. The night before the accident, I had seen Dana arguing with one of the women setting up the fair, and now it seemed she was being questioned by the police. She might have been arrested. I wondered what could possibly have happened, and hoped Dana would be released soon. Meanwhile, a rumour was spreading around the village that the fatality at the fair had been no accident but a deliberate murder. The police had set up a cordon to keep members of the public away from the site, but a few onlookers had lingered nearby and had finally been rewarded with a glimpse of a covered stretcher being carried into a waiting ambulance. Speculation was rife, but no one knew for certain whether it had been an accident or murder, and even Maud could not tell us the identity of the victim.

Forty-eight hours after the incident, the police issued a statement on the local news channel and in the paper, confirming that a woman had died at the fair in Ashton Mead on Saturday morning. The police extended their condolences to the family of the victim. The press release went on to state that the police were 'investigating the circumstances leading to the fatality', leaving the cause of death unspecified. The police statement prompted a further frenzy of speculation. Only a few people believed the victim had accidentally fallen from one of the rides. Most villagers were convinced she had been murdered.

Theories spread like wildfire around the village. Sitting with my friends, Hannah, Adam and Toby, in the pub that evening, we discussed the terrible incident. As far as we were aware, no one was missing from the village, which meant the victim had either been a visitor to the fair or else had belonged to it. The tragedy was on everyone's lips, along with accusations that were levelled at Dana Flack. By now, everyone knew she had been taken to the police station that morning and had not yet returned home. The outlook for her was looking bleak.

'There's no smoke without fire,' Cliff, the pub landlord, said, folding his fleshy arms across his stout belly. 'The police think Dana was up to something, and we know someone died. It all points in one direction.'

'We don't know they've accused Dana of anything,' I objected, although I knew he was making sense. 'We shouldn't make assumptions before we have all the facts. The chances are she witnessed an accident and is helping the police establish what happened.'

Hannah agreed with me. 'Don't forget I was taken in for questioning by the police not that long ago, and I was innocent,' she said. 'We don't know anything about what's going on with Dana.'

'We know someone's dead,' Toby pointed out. 'And we know Dana's been taken away by the police. She must at least be a suspect.'

Lying beside me, Poppy whimpered.

'Not necessarily,' I replied. 'They might not know yet what happened. They're investigating, which could mean anything. In any case, even if she's been arrested, that doesn't mean she's guilty. What happened to people being innocent until proven guilty?'

Everyone had an opinion, and the conversation grew quite heated. Some people were convinced Dana must have committed a murder, even though they had no evidence to back up their view, and we didn't even know yet whether anyone had actually been murdered. I kept fairly quiet, listening to the discussion with growing unease. Probably no one apart from me and Hannah knew that Dana had grown up on the fairground. Once that information became widely known, more people might be prepared to condemn her without good reason. Even if the police let her go, her chances of being accepted into the village community were looking more remote than ever.

'The trouble is, a lot of people think she doesn't really belong here, and that makes them quick to judge her,' Hannah said. 'They regard her as an outsider.'

Like me? I thought. And Richard? Lots of us didn't grow up here. And what about Adam? He's not been living here very long. Are we all outsiders who can be suspected of committing crimes just because we weren't born here?

'I'm not saying *I* think that,' Hannah added, seeing me scowling at her. 'But the locals don't know much about Dana, other than that she used to work for the local paper. And that didn't exactly make her popular. No one really knows her, and it's easier to judge a stranger harshly than a friend.' She sighed. 'People can be so narrow-minded.'

Dana had said something very similar, touching on the fairground community's myopic code. *Family loyalty means everything to showpeople.* The difference between Dana and these insular groups was that she had virtually no friends or family to support her. Exiled by her community and a stranger to the village, she was isolated as starkly as a hermit living in a remote cave in an uninhabited region. At least a hermit lived alone by choice. Dana was excluded from society against her will. Pity for my new friend suddenly overwhelmed me and tears threatened to choke my voice.

'We must do something to help her,' I blurted out. My friends turned to look at me. 'I mean,' I mumbled, 'she's all on her own and for all we know, she's done nothing wrong.'

'It's probably best not to get too involved,' Hannah replied uneasily. 'And in any case, what can we do? No one wants to cause trouble.' It wasn't clear if she was concerned about Dana, or about me. 'I'm sure the police will get to the truth of it and release her if she's innocent.'

'If it's true she's been arrested for murder, then why on earth would you want to help her? And like Hannah says, if she's not guilty then the police won't detain her for long,' Adam said. He paused to take a gulp of beer. 'I can't see what all the fuss is about.'

Lying by my feet, Poppy wagged her tail without opening her eyes. She wasn't bothered about Dana's arrest and, since no one had any food, she wasn't interested in our discussion. The conversation moved on to the safety issues at the fair. Passing our table and overhearing what we were saying, Cliff pointed out that we didn't yet know if the death could be blamed on a faulty ride. There could have been a murder. We had to concede that he had a point. Soon after that, Barry arrived. He raised a hand in greeting and Hannah beckoned him. He came over and offered to buy a round.

'You always get here after the rest of us and miss out on being bought a pint yourself, and then you always get in a round,' Toby said. 'I think it's my turn. Same again, everyone?'

Before Barry had taken a seat, we started bombarding him with questions.

'Well?' Hannah urged him. 'What can you tell us?'

'Hey, wait for me,' Toby protested as he stood up. 'I want to hear everything.'

Barry shrugged and looked round dejectedly. 'I'm sorry to disappoint you, but there's nothing to tell. Nothing you don't already know.' He leaned down to pet Poppy, who had woken up.

'We don't know anything,' Hannah complained.

'What about the victim?' Adam asked after a pause, when it was obvious Barry wasn't going to say anything else. 'What can you tell us?'

Barry didn't answer.

'Barry, tell us what you know,' Hannah insisted.

He finally straightened up from rubbing Poppy's belly. 'A woman was killed, tragically, at the fair at eleven on Saturday morning. Her identity has not been made public, as there hasn't yet been a formal identification.'

He lowered his voice. 'We believe the victim was working at the fair.'

'What have I missed? How did she die?' Toby asked, rejoining us with a tray of drinks.

Barry was still hovering.

'Aren't you going to sit down?' Hannah asked him after he had repeated what he had said, so Toby could hear.

'Actually,' Barry replied, looking slightly embarrassed, 'I came here to meet someone.'

Just then a girl I had never seen before walked into the bar, and he went over to greet her. He put his arm around her and brought her over to our table.

'This is Samantha,' he said, introducing all of us to his new girlfriend.

We made appropriate responses, and Hannah invited them to join us.

'There's plenty of room,' she insisted.

Adam jumped up and drew another chair over to our table while I studied Barry's new girlfriend covertly. Other than the fact that she was a girl, her resemblance to Barry was striking. Tall and slim, she had his protruding front teeth and his cheerful grin. In fact, judging on appearance alone, they seemed well suited. I was pleased for Barry, but couldn't kid myself that I wasn't also experiencing a sharp stab of disappointment. All of my friends seemed to be settling down: Hannah and Adam, Toby and the barmaid, Michelle, and now Barry had brought Samantha into our tight-knit circle. But there was no point in indulging in pointless regrets. It seemed Barry and me were never going to be an item, in spite of my recent change of heart. Alongside my other emotions, I felt an overwhelming sense of relief that I had said nothing to Hannah about my burgeoning interest in him.

Dismissing my secret chagrin, I tried to pay attention to the conversation. Hannah was asking how Barry and Samantha had met, and she was telling us all to call her Sam. It didn't soften my disappointment to register that she seemed friendly, and Hannah obviously liked her. Determined to keep my feelings about Samantha to myself, I struggled against my resentment. If Hannah suspected me of being jealous, she would never stop reminding me I had brought this situation on myself by rejecting Barry for so long. 'You had your chance,' she would say, and knowing she was right wouldn't make the circumstances any easier to bear.

Beside Dana's problems mine seemed trivial, and that night my thoughts turned from my own selfish disappointment to Dana, incarcerated in a police cell. I lay awake for a long time, turning over in my mind everything she had ever said to me. She had grown up on the fair, which was unsettling in itself, given that someone had died there while it was in Ashton Mead, not long after she had recently relocated to the village. The timing of the death, while Dana was living in Ashton Mead, certainly seemed coincidental. Equally worrying was the argument I had witnessed between Dana and one of the fairground women, the day before the tragedy occurred. Worst of all, Dana had told me someone had been murdered before the police issued their statement. If there had been a murder, Dana mentioning it before anyone else heard about it suggested she might actually be guilty. At the very least, she must know more than she had told me. I wondered whether it was possible she was involved, and whether I ought to tell anyone what she had said to me. But she had spoken to me in confidence, and there was no way I wanted to become an accessory to a crime, if she was actually guilty, which I doubted. In any case, there was really very little I could tell the police. Before I did anything, I needed to speak to Dana again.

With such worrying thoughts churning round in my mind, when I did drift off, my sleep was disturbed by nightmares. In one, I was chased across the fair by a dark-eyed man who was dragging a screaming woman behind him. As the back of her head bumped horribly against the running boards of a hideous ghost train, I saw that in place of one of her eyeballs there was only a mess of blood. Her other eye fixed on me, accusingly, and I called out her name, 'Dana'. For once, I was pleased when Poppy's barking woke me before it was time to get up.

4

THAT MORNING, WALKING POPPY to Jane's house, I thought about Dana all alone in a cell, and wished there was something I could do to help her. It was a beautiful sunny day, which somehow made the idea of being locked up indoors seem even more upsetting. The thought of not being able to walk in the fresh air, enjoying the sights and smells of summer, was almost unbearable. Poppy loved being outside and spent so long sniffing the various grassy verges and trees, not to mention weeds proliferating at the edge of the pavement, that in the end I had to hurry her along or risk being late for work. Hannah was always understanding if I was delayed, but that made me even more resolved to be on time so as not to take advantage of her good nature.

Preoccupied with her dog, Jane was the only person I met who didn't seem interested in the recent tragedy. Holly had become very frail recently, and there was no doubt she was physically deteriorating. She opened her eyes a fraction when Poppy nuzzled the side of her head and thumped her tail wearily before going back to sleep.

'Everything seems to be too much effort for her,' Jane sighed, nearly in tears. She reached down to stroke the old dog whose eyelids didn't even flicker in acknowledgement. 'She's stopped eating altogether. I don't know what to do. I've tried all sorts of things to tempt her, but she just lies there and refuses to eat. She won't even move. All she wants to do is sleep.'

Poppy laid down beside her old friend, whimpering softly, and Holly's tail wagged feebly in response.

'It's like she's just given up,' Jane said. 'I feel like she's slipping away from me. I'm afraid I'm losing her.' She covered her face in her hands.

Feeling helpless, I urged her to take Holly to the vet. 'Maybe she's ill? They might be able to do something for her.'

But we both knew what the problem was; the most skilful vet in the world could do nothing about her dog's advanced age, and I understood Jane's reluctance to hear what a vet might have to say. I offered to take Poppy to work with me, but Jane insisted on Poppy staying. Holly seemed to find her presence comforting.

'She doesn't seem to be uncomfortable,' Jane added. 'If she was in pain or suffering, I'd take her straight to the vet. But–' she broke off with a sigh. 'I just want to keep her a little longer. Just a few more days. Is that selfish of me? I can't bear to lose her.' She began to cry.

'It's not selfish at all. It's perfectly understandable. And you never know, she might rally.'

Poppy reached out and placed one of her little paws on Holly's neck. Following her example, I put my arm around Jane who laid her head on my shoulder and sobbed quietly. When I left, the sunshine seemed less bright.

'How was mum?' Hannah asked me when I arrived at the tea shop.

I shrugged, and we both sighed. I held back from mentioning that Dana had told me there had been a murder. Reluctant to share my worst fears with anyone, even Hannah, I was afraid I might be regarded as an accessory to murder. My situation felt horribly complicated, and the best course of action seemed to be to say nothing, at least for the time being. In different circumstances, I might have asked Barry for his opinion. As a police officer, he should be able to advise me. But it would be difficult to consult him without revealing what Dana had told me, and I didn't want to betray her trust. Unwilling to alert Hannah to my suspicions, I decided to see if it was possible for me to visit Dana and try to ascertain what had happened at the fair, and whether she might be implicated in murder. It would be a huge relief if Dana could convince me of her innocence. I really liked her, and was keen to reassure myself that she had not killed anyone, in spite of rumours to the contrary.

Meanwhile, Hannah had other matters on her mind. She wanted to know what I thought about Holly, and I had to admit that in my opinion the old dog was dying. We agreed it was going to be difficult for Jane, but there was nothing we could do to save Holly. Hannah broke down in tears just thinking about it.

'I've known her since she was a few weeks old,' she said, wiping her eyes. 'But still, like you say, there's nothing we can do. Let's talk about something else. What did you think of Samantha?'

Of course, Hannah had no idea that my feelings for Barry had changed, and I was proud of myself for talking enthusiastically about how friendly Samantha was, and how happy Barry seemed with her. The subject was a sensitive one for me, and I was pleased when the bell rang to signal the arrival of customers. At least Hannah had cheered up when she stopped thinking about Holly. With everything that was going on, we didn't even mention Dana, but I was obliged to listen to customers discussing her throughout the day. The consensus of local opinion seemed to be that Dana had been arrested and would very soon be convicted of murder.

'And to think she's been living among us,' one old woman said, as if Dana was an alien from another planet.

'And reporting on everyone's business in that newspaper of hers,' her companion replied acidly. 'That kind of gossip can be very harmful,' she added, oblivious to the irony of her words.

There was little sympathy for poor Dana, at least from the customers at the tea shop. I went home, feeling guilty at my failure to make any attempt to defend her. The following morning, unable to bear the uncertainty any longer, I requested time off work to go and see her. Somehow I had to compel Dana to tell me the truth. With a show of reluctance, Hannah agreed to let me go.

'Don't stay there a moment longer than necessary,' she said. 'You know how busy we get. I'm paying you to wait at tables, not to take suspected criminals under your wing.'

Since the murder at the fair, the tea shop had been consistently packed, as excited villagers gathered to exchange views and gossip. No one spoke up for Dana, and I was careful to keep my opinion to myself. Unsure what to believe, I decided not to stick my neck out in her defence. No one was going to listen to me, and if I wasn't careful I might end up causing trouble for myself, without helping Dana. The police certainly appeared to think Dana might be guilty. Conscious of my status as a relative newcomer to Ashton Mead, I knew that while many locals accepted me into their community, especially those who had been acquainted with my great aunt, many others barely tolerated me. I hadn't exactly been joking in telling Dana she might have to wait fifty years before she could be fully assimilated into the community.

I set off quite early in the morning, and an hour later was waiting in the police station to see if they would allow me to speak to Dana. Time crawled by as I sat there, kicking my heels. I was beginning to regret my rash decision to take time off work to go there, when at last Dana walked in, looking very pale and utterly exhausted.

'To be honest, I'm relieved it's you,' she admitted as she sat down. 'Can you believe I nearly refused to leave my cell? I wasn't sure who it was.' She smiled uneasily. 'I was afraid Alfie had sent someone.'

'Alfie? What do you mean?'

She gave me a curious glance. 'I believe the police are questioning him as we speak, but he'll wriggle his way out of trouble like he always does. He was supposed to be getting married to Paris, the woman who was killed, so they'll have to speak to him, I suppose. But it'll be pointless, really, because he'll just lie and convince them he had nothing to do with her death. He can be very persuasive when he wants to be. I should know. It took me long enough to see him for what he really is.'

'I expect you were young,' I murmured.

Dana pulled a face. 'Yes, he likes young girls.'

It sounded to me as though Dana knew more than she had yet admitted, and I asked her to tell me more about him.

'He's not someone you want to have anything to do with, not if you have any sense,' she replied firmly. 'I should know.' She glanced around and lowered her voice. 'We were supposed to be getting married, me and Alfie, but I suppose you could say I grew out of my infatuation.' She gave a hollow laugh. 'He was furious when I plucked up the courage to tell him I wanted to leave him, and he never forgave me. It's basically down to him that I had to leave the fair, and I've been ostracised by the travelling community ever since. Alfie made sure they all regard me as a traitor, but it wasn't like that. It's true some people leave and start blabbing about things best left at home, but that was never my intention. When it came to it, I just wanted to go, with no hard feelings, and no recriminations. In a way, I was lucky because my parents made sure I had a proper education. They sent me away to a boarding school when I was thirteen. I stuck it for three years, and that stood me in good stead when I needed to get a job outside the fair. But Alfie dragged my name through the mud and made sure I was exiled from the travelling community.'

'Did you want to leave?' I asked her.

'Leave my home and my family and everyone I knew? No.' She shook her head to emphasise her point. 'I didn't want to leave. It was hard. But it was worth it to get away from him. In the end I felt I didn't really have a choice. He threatened to kill me, and he probably would have, if I hadn't got away from him.'

'Why didn't you tell other people there about his threats? Surely they wouldn't put up with him if they knew what he's like.'

'You know, I didn't even bother to try to expose the truth about him, because I knew no one would listen to me. When all's said and done, he's one of them, and I'm not. Not anymore.' She sighed. 'They close ranks, treat the police with suspicion, and don't trust anyone who's not one of them. Besides, Alfie took over when my dad died, and he runs the show. The rest of the community rely on him for their livelihood.'

'Surely it doesn't have to be him,' I said. 'Can't someone else be in charge?'

She shook her head. 'Only by ousting Alfie, and Alfie likes to be top dog. He wouldn't tolerate anyone trying to undermine him. They need him, and I was expendable. But there's more to it than that. Alfie has a way of compelling people to do what he wants, regardless of their own feelings.'

'What about the victim?' I asked. 'What do you know about her?'

Hesitantly, I told her that I thought I might have seen Alfie at the fair, not long before the alleged murder took place. Of course, I couldn't be sure the man I had seen was Dana's former boyfriend, but I was almost certain I had heard the woman call him Alfie. Dana asked me to describe him and nodded when I told her. The man I had seen was very good looking, with a fit body, classically handsome face, and beautiful dark eyes.

Dana nodded. 'That sounds like Alfie,' she said, with a grim smile. 'But don't be fooled by his looks. He's a vicious thug, and a narcissist. He never forgave me for walking out on him. He didn't care about my leaving the fair, and my family and everyone I knew, he only cared that I might dent his reputation by leaving him. You see, in Alfie's world view, everyone is in love with him, and I was lucky to be chosen by him. Not that he was faithful, but in his mind that was perfectly acceptable. Alfie lives by his own rules and according to him he should be free to do whatever he likes. I was supposed to fall in line and accept any meagre crumbs of affection he doled out. Like he was an emperor.' She laughed bitterly. 'It's hard to believe I was taken in by him. Anyway, once I decided to leave him, that's when the serious abuse started. He seemed to think he could literally beat me into submission.' She smiled grimly. 'It didn't work. Usually he was careful to injure me where no one could see, but one time he was careless and hit me in the face and broke my nose. He denied it, of course. He said I was lying when I told everyone what had happened.'

'That sounds terrible. I'm so sorry,' I stammered. It was difficult to know what else to say.

I felt mortified at having found Alfie attractive, and was impressed with Poppy for warning me not to trust him. I wondered how she was, and whether Holly had regained any strength.

'As long as he gets everything he wants, Alfie is nice as can be,' Dana said. 'He could charm the fleas off a hedgehog. But if anyone dares to cross him—' she rolled her eyes and exhaled sharply. 'That's when he turns. Seriously, he's a psycho. He's completely unhinged. His temper is off the scale. And he can flip in a second. He's the reason I left the fair. I told the police he must have killed Paris, but they're not going to take my word for it. He'll get them to dismiss anything I say as the ravings of a jealous ex-girlfriend. But I'm sure it was him. Poor Paris. I knew her.' She sighed. 'She was still a child when I left the fair, and she can't have been much older than eighteen when she died. She was far too young for Alfie, but he was the boss of the fair and I suppose she was infatuated with him, like I once was. The thing that's really bothering me is that I can't help wondering whether I could have done more to stop him. Do you think I could have prevented him from mistreating another poor girl? That's the question that's tormenting me. Could I have stopped this from happening, if I had spoken out instead of running away?'

Wondering whether Paris was the girl I had seen talking to Alfie, I was about to ask Dana to describe her, but there was no time. With tears in her eyes, Dana thanked me for visiting her.

'You're the only person who's been to see me,' she added in a low voice. 'Even my own mother doesn't dare come.'

She didn't explain why that was. Wondering if it was true that Alfie exerted so powerful an influence on all the fairground workers, I left, promising to visit her again soon.

'Will I see you tomorrow?' she asked, suddenly looking forlorn.

It was difficult to promise that. It took me the best part of an hour to get to Swindon if the bus arrived in Ashton Mead on time, which wasn't always the case. Basically, visiting the police station meant I was away from the tea shop for nearly three hours, but I promised to do my best to return the next day. With Dana's murmured thanks echoing in my ears, I hurried to the bus stop. It had been sunny when I set out, so I hadn't bothered to wear a coat. Although it was a warm day, the sky was overcast by the time I left the police station, and it looked as though it might rain. I was relieved when my bus arrived, and even happier to be back at the tea shop.

'How was it?' Hannah asked me after we closed and were clearing up later that afternoon.

With a sigh, I admitted that the visit had been quite depressing. What with Holly growing so weak, and Dana in prison, it had been a miserable day. It was raining quite heavily when I left the tea shop to collect Poppy. Having left my coat at home, I was soon drenched, which did nothing to improve my mood.

'At least it's not cold out,' I said, when Jane insisted on lending me a waterproof jacket.

There was not much point in my accepting her offer since I was already wet through, but Jane insisted I borrow it. I carried Poppy underneath the jacket because she hated getting wet. At last we reached our front door; I had never been happier to be home.

5

WHILE THE MURDER INVESTIGATION was ongoing, the fairground folk were not allowed to leave the village. Individual showmen could easily sneak away under cover of darkness, but the police refused permission for any of the rides and stalls to be moved from the riverside pitch. All of the vehicles and equipment were effectively grounded until the police relaxed their restrictions. Clearly the police did not trust the showmen to comply with the request, because both exit routes from the village were regularly patrolled by police cars. In any case, if any of the caravans or lorries and trailers left the area, they would be tracked and brought back. As far as we could tell, none of the fairground workers attempted to make a break for it. Instead, they stayed put and fretted at their enforced immobilisation. We overheard several heated discussions between police officers and fairground workers. The latter insisted on being allowed to move on to their next stop, while the police doggedly advised them against trying to leave.

Hannah and I hardly saw our friend, Barry, during this period while the fairground workers were being held in limbo. As the only police officer resident in Ashton

Mead, he seemed to be permanently on duty. On the rare occasions when he popped into the pub to say a quick hello and down a pint, he looked exhausted.

'I don't mind,' he assured us, stifling a yawn. 'Obviously I'd prefer not to be working such long hours, but it's all part of the job and I wouldn't change it for anything.' He even admitted that he was finding it all quite exciting. 'At least something's happening.'

'That "something" happens to be a murder enquiry,' Hannah pointed out acerbically. 'It's hardly the kind of excitement most people would go for. For most of us, a holiday or a birthday is enough.'

Barry gave her a tolerant smile. He had known Hannah since they were children, and he was by nature slow to take offence.

'You know what I mean,' he replied mildly.

I wanted to know if Barry was still seeing his new girlfriend, but was wary of betraying my interest. Hannah had no such reservations. She enquired after Samantha and Barry responded with a grin.

'She's great,' he said.

Every now and then we caught sight of him driving along the High Street with a fellow police officer, and Poppy and I occasionally spotted him talking to showpeople near the site of the fairground. The big wheel hung motionless against the skyline, the helter skelter had been dismantled, and the rides were all silent, waiting to be disassembled and transported to their next location. It was like a ghostly impression of the lively bustling fair. Throughout the village, the atmosphere was tense. Living very close to where the fairground community was corralled, I was glad to have Poppy for company, especially overnight. She seemed cowed by the presence of so many strangers in the neighbourhood, and whimpered in her sleep more often than usual. I hoped she wasn't disturbed by Holly's failing health.

Since Maud's recent marriage to the local butcher, Barry had moved into her flat above her shop. As her nephew and unofficially adopted son, he had grown up in that flat. It must have felt strange for him to be back in his childhood home, living there on his own. It crossed my mind that he might not be alone there, but neither Hannah nor I had seen anything of his new girlfriend in the village, so I assumed she wasn't living with him. Not yet, at least. Meanwhile, Barry seemed to be busy working. Selfishly, I hoped his dedication to his job would put Samantha off him. When he wasn't patrolling the streets in uniform, he generally stationed himself in Maud's shop. She claimed to be pleased that the fairground folk were staying around, since they brought their custom to her store. At the same time, she complained that they were inclined to be rowdy and even light-fingered, especially the youngsters, and she had to constantly watch out for shoplifters. Barry, tall and bearing the authority of a police officer even when he was off duty, was a welcome presence in her shop. Whether or not they recognised him out of his uniform, strangers seemed to respect him. According to Maud, the behaviour of young lads from the fair noticeably improved whenever he was around.

Hannah and I were relieved that the fairground workers avoided the tea shop. They might have temporarily increased our takings, but if they deterred our regular customers from coming in, the damage could prove significant in the long term. The pub was a different story. A sizeable group of showpeople was often in there, drinking and chatting. They were clearly frustrated, but they kept to themselves, aware that not everyone welcomed their presence in the village. As long as they caused no disturbance, Cliff was happy to encourage them to keep drinking. Within a few days, they had become a familiar, if not a welcome, sight in the village. Most of the locals were soon resigned to their presence. In any case, we knew it could not last long.

We were busy in the tea shop so I did not return to Swindon the day after my visit to the police station, but was planning to ask permission to take time off the following day to go and see Dana. As it turned out, I didn't have a chance to visit her at the police station again. The first I knew of her release was when she appeared outside the tea shop early in the morning, about half an hour before we were due to open. Pottering about laying tables and preparing for the breakfast rush, I didn't notice her standing on the pavement, waiting for us to open. Hannah was in the kitchen taking a tray of freshly baked scones out of the oven, when Poppy suddenly ran past her, narrowly missing knocking her off balance. Swerving around me, and barking furiously, she raced past me to the street door. Looking round, I saw Dana waiting outside, and hurried over to let her in.

After the initial warm greetings, I brought her a tray of breakfast and she tucked in as though she had not eaten for days.

'This is good,' she kept repeating as she scooped up another mouthful of egg, or stabbed another sausage with her fork. 'This is so good.'

Although, strictly speaking, customers were not allowed to give Poppy food from their plates, many of our regulars slipped her crumbs and other titbits, especially when they thought no one was looking. Fortunately, other customers never complained. Poppy knew how to look irresistible when she was begging silently for treats. Dana was particularly generous with Poppy, and I was not the only one who was pleased when Dana came straight to the tea shop on her release from custody. Not everyone was equally happy to see her back in Ashton Mead. Several of the villagers sniffed disapprovingly as they passed her table, and darted censorious glances in her direction when they sat down. The atmosphere in the tea shop was charged with such latent hostility, I was afraid Hannah might ask Dana to leave.

Hannah shook her head when I asked her what she intended to do.

'No one's leaving, are they?' she replied.

Hannah was right. Dana's presence did not seem to be discouraging customers. If anything, we were busier than usual. Our regular customers sat watching Dana surreptitiously, probably all listening out for any morsels of news she let slip. In between taking orders, I sat with Dana for a moment, ignoring the scowls of several customers.

'I don't think everyone is happy about me being here,' Dana whispered. 'In fact, if this was a few hundred years ago, I'd probably have been lynched by now, and be swinging from the nearest tree, if not burning at the stake. At the very least I'd be in the stocks having rotten tomatoes chucked at me.' She laughed mirthlessly. 'Thank goodness we live in civilised times,' she added sourly, glancing around at the customers who were staring at her.

Unlike many of the villagers, Poppy was happy to see Dana again. Lying down underneath her table, she refused to budge.

'Poppy's lying on my foot,' Dana told me, beaming.

'She's probably trying to stop you leaving again, or she could be feeling protective towards you,' I said. 'In any case, it's definitely a sign of affection.'

'I'm glad someone likes me,' Dana answered with a sigh.

'It's not that bad, is it?'

'Well, if you call being homeless "not that bad" then no.'

She must have seen I was surprised, because she explained that her landlord had given her notice. She did not have to move out immediately, but she had to be gone by the end of the month which only gave her two weeks to find alternative accommodation.

'I think he suspects I'll be leaving anyway,' she added. 'I mean, if I'm convicted of murder.'

'Is that likely? They've let you go, haven't they?'

She nodded before confiding in an undertone that the police had repeatedly accused her of murder and had pressed her to admit her guilt. That was outrageous, she added, seeing as she was innocent, but the police had implied they were convinced she was guilty and told her she would receive better treatment if she confessed. At last, in the absence of any evidence linking her to the scene, and unable to force a confession out of her, they had no choice but to let her go. And now, she concluded, she was going to be homeless.

'I might as well have confessed to a crime I didn't commit,' she told me crossly. 'At least that way I'd have a roof over my head. In the end, the only thing that prevented me from caving in to the pressure was that my false confession would have stopped them looking for the real killer. And the last thing I want is for him to get away with it.'

Dana explained that her landlord had given her a lame excuse about his cousin coming to the area, meaning that he needed her to vacate her room, but Dana was convinced she was being evicted because of the murder investigation. What was clear was that her landlord no longer wanted her in his property. He was keen to be rid of her as soon as possible so he could let the room to someone who was not only less controversial, but also more likely to stay for a while. Seeing Poppy sleeping so comfortably on Dana's foot, I reached a snap decision. Had I thought it through, I might not have suggested Dana come and stay with me, but all I could think was that Dana was being thrown out, and someone had to come to her aid. Almost as soon as the words left my lips, I felt a flutter of regret, but before I had a chance to reconsider my offer, Dana was already thanking me with tears in her eyes.

'I never dreamed anyone could be so kind. Thank you, thank you. I can't tell you how grateful I am. I'll take Poppy for walks and keep the place clean,' she gushed. 'You're the kindest person I've ever met outside of the fair.'

Instead of experiencing a warm glow as a result of my generosity, I was aware only of feeling slightly shocked by my audacious gesture, and uneasy about my new tenant.

Hannah was taken aback when I told her. 'She's in trouble with the police. They questioned her about a murder,' she protested.

'They let her go without charging her with anything.'

'Are you sure what you're doing is sensible? You don't know the first thing about her.'

'I know she worked for the Swindon News for years,' I replied.

'And now she's unemployed. How is she going to afford to pay you any rent? If it's about money, Emily, I know I haven't given you a raise since you started–'

'It's got nothing to do with money. She's in trouble and she's a friend.'

'Since when did you and Dana become so close?'

I shrugged and muttered that we had met several times for a drink, but I held back from mentioning what Dana had told me about Alfie. She hadn't exactly mentioned her suspicions to me in confidence, but it seemed best not to tell anyone, not even my closest friend. Hannah was bound to talk about it with her boyfriend, Adam, and possibly Barry would hear about it. He might pass the information on to his Aunt Maud who was an incorrigible gossip. In no time, everyone in the village would know all about Dana's past, no doubt with a few extravagant embellishments added in each reiteration.

Hannah stared at me, nonplussed. 'You complained she was always poking her nose in where it wasn't wanted. You couldn't stand her when she was a news reporter. How are you going to cope with her living in your house?'

I shrugged. 'We'll manage,' was all I could come up with.

'You don't know anything about her,' Hannah insisted.

'Of course, I do,' I protested. 'I'm not a complete idiot.' *And you're not my mother*, I thought, but didn't say.

'Well? What do you know about her?'

'I know she's my friend.'

'Emily,' Hannah said sternly, 'the police seem to suspect she murdered someone. How safe are you going to be with her sleeping under your roof?'

'Poppy trusts her,' I said, feeling my confidence fade.

'Oh, and Poppy knows she's not dangerous?'

As it happened, I had always found Poppy a very reliable judge of character, but that was not to say she couldn't be wrong. Perhaps she was blinded by Dana giving her treats. But I had issued the invitation and couldn't retract it.

'Tell her you have someone else coming to stay,'

'No, I'm not going to lie to her. I told you, we're friends and she's in trouble. I'm going to stand by her whatever happens. I'd do the same for you.'

'What if the police find proof she killed that woman at the fair?'

'Then you'll have the satisfaction of saying "I told you so".'

'Not if she's killed you first.'

'She's not going to kill me. That's a ridiculous thing to say.'

All the same, I couldn't help feeling nervous.

'I suppose it's understandable,' Hannah said, looking at me sadly. 'Dana's got more in common with you than I have.'

'Don't be silly,' I replied, 'You know what it's like to be single, and I've been in relationships, even if they didn't turn out so well.'

'That's not what I meant,' she said. 'You and Dana have both lived in other places. She must have visited lots of different towns, and you lived in London, for goodness' sake. I've only ever really lived here, in the village. Ashton Mead is all I've known. I've never experienced anything else, or had an opportunity to reinvent myself and change my life. I've always lived in a familiar setting, among people who know me.'

'What about when you were married?' I asked her.

'For all of five months,' she replied, 'and most of it was more of a holiday than anything else. We went to America for an extended honeymoon, and after that we went to live in his massive house in the country, but I've never actually lived in a town or any other village. It's not the same for you and Dana. You have a different outlook on life.'

'It's not that different,' I said, although she had a point. 'And you're still my best friend.'

That night, Poppy stretched out across the bottom of my bed where she liked to sleep, by my feet.

'Oh Poppy, what have you got me into?' I murmured, reaching forward to stroke her head.

She wagged her tail as if to reassure me that everything would be fine.

'Oh, what do you know? You're only a dog,' I said.

With a baleful glare, she jumped off the bed and went to sleep in her little basket under the window.

6

THAT EVENING I HURRIEDLY dusted and hoovered the spare room and changed the sheets which had been on the bed since my mother's last visit. I didn't have another matching set but, given the circumstances, Dana wasn't going to mind sleeping on a pink sheet under a yellow and white striped duvet cover, with a pale blue pillowcase. Having finished remaking the bed, I put a clean set of towels on it and replaced the worn sliver of soap in the bathroom with a new bar. My excitement at having a friend to stay intensified, as did my nerves. I liked Dana, and admired her toughness, but Hannah's words nagged at me. *The police seem to think she murdered someone. How safe are you going to be with her sleeping under your roof?*

I offered to help Dana move her stuff, but she assured me that she could manage everything herself. When she moved in the next evening, I saw that was true. I did my best to hide my surprise on seeing how little she brought with her. A medium-sized suitcase on wheels for her clothes, no larger than one I might pack for a weekend away, and a backpack with a few books and her monitor and keyboard and chargers for her iPad and phone, were all she had. There were no cooking pots or implements, not even any writing materials. She told me she had recorded all her material for the newspaper electronically, and I remembered seeing her taking notes on her phone. It was hard to believe anyone could manage with so few belongings, but I supposed travelling light was a way of life she had developed while she was living an itinerant life as a fairground child.

Instead of going to the pub that evening, we decided to stay in and I offered to cook. My culinary skills were basic but I managed to rustle up a decent spaghetti bolognese which Dana pretended to enjoy. She didn't eat much, claiming she was still full from her breakfast that morning at the tea shop. We opened a bottle of wine which we finished after dinner, with an assortment of Hannah's scones and cupcakes for dessert. While Dana had only picked at my spaghetti bolognese, she scoffed Hannah's baking. By the time we finished, we were both feeling comfortably stuffed. Even Poppy went to sleep, her little belly bloated from a plate of her favourite dog food doused in bolognese sauce. Relaxed from gorging ourselves, we allowed the conversation to drift to the subject we had been avoiding all evening.

'What made the police arrest you, and why did they let you go?' I asked, leaning back in my chair and putting my feet up on a footstool.

'They let me go because they didn't have a shred of evidence to suggest I might have killed someone,' she answered, a trifle tartly.

'But why did they arrest you at all?'

'They didn't arrest me, they took me in for questioning,' she replied. 'But you're probably wondering what made them suspect me in the first place,' she added, her defensive tone evaporating. 'No smoke without fire, I know, I get it.' She took a sip of her wine. 'I'll tell you exactly what happened, and then if you want to ask me to leave, I'll go at once.'

Poppy sat up and whimpered as I waited in silence to hear Dana's story.

'The police had nothing to go on, until one of the showmen accused me of murder.'

'That was Alfie, wasn't it?' I blurted out.

She nodded. 'The rest of them said nothing, even though they must know I'm innocent. What you have to understand is that I'm a useful scapegoat. The fairground community lives in fear of the authorities. They're never popular with mainstream society, and public opinion can turn against them at the drop of a hat. Everyone loves the fair, but no one likes the people who bring it to them. That's why they stick together. Some of them have had it in for me ever since I left, and I can't say I altogether blame them. But I'm not the only one who's chosen to quit the travelling community. It happens. Usually everyone understands. Alfie was the only one who took the rejection personally when I left. It was an affront to his pride, even though he was the reason I left.' She paused as if there was more she wanted to say, then she sighed. 'And now you're the only friend I have.'

Poppy opened her eyes and let out a single bark and Dana laughed. 'I meant you in the plural, of course,' she said, and Poppy wagged her tail.

'You're my only friend, and even you aren't sure whether to trust a single word I say. It's true, isn't it? You're wondering why on earth you let me into your home. You're asking yourself if I'm going to murder you in your bed tonight.'

Poppy let out another indignant bark and we both laughed.

'If I didn't trust you, why would I have invited you to stay with me?' I protested, laughing in an attempt to cover up my embarrassment at having harboured those suspicions, even fleetingly. 'I'm sorry,' I added, 'this can't be funny for you. I'm just a bit pissed.'

'You invited me to stay because you jump in without thinking,' she replied seriously. 'I expect that's got you into trouble before now. I dare say this isn't the first time you've trusted someone on a whim?'

That was true. In the past I had been taken in by people preying on my gullibility. Poppy seemed to sense which of my friends were honest and principled, and who was setting out to deceive me. I trusted Poppy's instincts more than my own, and she clearly liked Dana.

'Life is risky,' I replied. 'But if we never trusted anyone else, we might as well all be hermits, living all alone in a remote cave. I don't want to live like that. I like having friends, and I want you to be one of them. Do I have to give you a reason for liking you?'

'You *are* drunk,' she said, but I could tell she was pleased.

As if to prove her point, I reached out to pet Poppy and slid off my chair. As I lay on the floor, giggling helplessly, Poppy leaped on top of me and began licking my face. All at once, I felt a wave of happiness wash through me. I was the fortunate owner of a beautiful cottage, my wonderful little dog was my constant and loyal companion, and now Poppy and I had a new friend – as long as Dana wasn't convicted of murder. That was a sobering proviso, and I shoved it to the back of my mind as Dana extended a hand to help me up from the floor.

My phone rang and I was not surprised to hear Hannah's voice. She sounded unnaturally tense. 'I'm just calling to say you can come in half an hour later tomorrow, if you like,' she said, giving what was obviously a trumped up excuse for calling me to check everything was all right.

'Why's that?' I asked. 'Are you opening late?' We both knew that wasn't the reason for her call. 'Don't worry,' I added, with a laugh. 'Dana hasn't murdered me in my bed yet.'

Muttering crossly that the thought hadn't entered her head, Hannah rang off. When I grumbled about Hannah's fussing, Dana's response surprised me.

'Perhaps you should ask her over, or arrange to go out together, or something,' Dana suggested. 'Don't you think she might be feeling excluded? You've been best friends for a long time, haven't you, and now I've moved in with you. It might sound daft, but maybe she's feeling a bit jealous?'

As I lay in bed that night, waiting to fall asleep, I mulled over what Hannah had said about my having more in common with Dana than with her. It was true Hannah and I were close. We spent almost every day in each other's company, working together and socialising, and I thought of her as my best friend. Given that she was very happy with Adam, it would never have occurred to me that she might be jealous of my new friendship with Dana. But once the possibility had been raised, it made sense, and I resolved to be more attentive to Hannah in future. My relationship with Dana might not last long. Once the murder enquiry was wrapped up, she would probably want to move on with her life and there was nothing to keep her in Ashton Mead where most people had judged her harshly. My friendship with Hannah was hopefully for life, unless something went badly wrong. It was strange to reflect that Hannah might be feeling possessive towards me. Thinking about Hannah, and how important her friendship was to me, I lay there listening to Poppy snuffling softly in her sleep until I drifted into dreamless slumber.

The next morning, I arrived at the tea shop a few minutes early, having dropped Poppy at Jane's house to spend the day with Holly. Dana had offered to look after her, but she was still asleep when I left for work. I didn't want to wake her, and it didn't seem fair on her or Poppy to leave them together unannounced, without having filled Dana in on Poppy's routine. Somehow, leaving Poppy with her would make her move into Rosecroft seem more definite, and I had decided to take things slowly. Besides, Holly seemed to find Poppy's company comforting, even if the old dog was asleep most of the time. I was also concerned to pay attention to Hannah's feelings, and she had made it clear she was apprehensive about my rushing into a friendship with Dana. If nothing else, I at least wanted to show my respect for Hannah's opinion. Neither of us mentioned her offer to let me come into work late that morning and we opened up as usual and spent a busy morning serving breakfasts.

Hannah and I didn't mention Dana at all that day, although she was probably in both of our minds. It was difficult not to think about her, as most of our customers seemed to be talking about nothing else but the murder and the possible suspects.

'It was probably someone from the fair,' was the most commonly expressed opinion.

'But why did the police arrest Dana Flack?' was a question that came up again and again.

I wanted to point out that she had not been arrested, only taken in for questioning, after the real culprit had accused her in order to draw the heat away from himself. But I held back from attempting to defend Dana in public. Before long, everyone in the village would know she had moved in with me. In the meantime, I was in no rush to divulge that information. I shuddered to think what scandalous rumours might circulate once the villagers discovered Dana had exchanged a prison cell for a bed at Rosecroft. Dimly I began to see the wisdom of Hannah's advice. A good name is easy to lose but hard to regain, as Shakespeare pointed out. In an excess of sympathy for Dana's plight, I had heedlessly risked my reputation, without a thought for how it might impact Hannah. At the time my invitation had felt like a selfless gesture, but I was beginning to realise that in some ways it had actually been quite selfish. I hoped it would not put customers off coming to the tea shop. Hannah had been a good friend to me, and it worried me to think I might have repaid her kindness by harming her business.

'Isn't your mother coming to see you sometime soon?' Hannah asked me, when we stopped for a bite of lunch between the lunchtime rush and teatime when we were always busy.

'What's that?'

With a sinking feeling, I remembered that my mother had arranged to visit me, and she was due to turn up that day. It was half past two. She had probably already arrived on the midday bus. Since she had not appeared in the tea shop, she had probably gone to Rosecroft to drop off her bag, and stayed there. She knew the unoriginal hiding place under a flowerpot in my front garden where I kept a spare key to the cottage. Usually I looked forward to her visits, and prepared for them by stocking the fridge, tidying the kitchen and the living room, cleaning the bathroom and checking there were clean sheets on the spare bed. In my preoccupation with the fair, the murder, and Dana, I had completely forgotten about her. The cottage was a mess, the spare bed was occupied, my fridge was almost empty and, worse than anything else, instead of me she would have found a suspected murderer in the cottage. Had I remembered her planned visit, I would have postponed it. As it was, she could not have turned up at a worse time.

'What am I going to do about her?' I wailed.

Hannah shrugged. 'You wanted to invite Dana into your home. You have to deal with the consequences. I just hope your thoughtless decision won't put people off coming to the tea shop, once they find out my waitress is fraternising with a suspected murderer.'

'That's harsh,' I objected, even though I had harboured the same apprehension myself.

'I'm only thinking of my business,' she replied. 'The tea shop has a reputation to maintain, and my customers want to feel comfortable here.'

The ramifications of what I had believed was a selfless gesture to help a homeless woman were impossible to ignore. Life had never seemed so complicated before, nor so daunting. Not only did Hannah feel I had let her down, but my mother would be waiting for me at home, and I dreaded to think what she would have to say about the situation. A simple impulse to be helpful, and my whole world had come crashing down around me. Thinking things through had never been my forte, but this time my rash decision threatened to affect other people as well as me, and I cursed myself for being so impetuous. The one bright spot in my life was Poppy. At least she wouldn't lecture me about my thoughtless choices. In any case, she was partly to blame for my current plight, because it was partly her attitude that had persuaded me to trust Dana. And if Dana turned out to be innocent, as I suspected, we would have been right to trust her and offer her a lifeline when she was being thrown out on the street. If she was guilty, and my mother had entered Rosecroft oblivious of the potential risk, my mother's life might be in danger.

'I have to go,' I blurted out and ran out of the tea shop, without waiting for Hannah's reaction.

Without stopping to collect Poppy from Jane's house, I sprinted all the way home, praying that nothing terrible had happened in my absence. My chest hurt by the time I reached Rosecroft. Panting and trembling I opened the door, hoping to hear my mother chatting with Dana. The cottage was silent.

7

As THE FRONT DOOR slammed shut behind me, I heard my mother's voice calling out.

'Emily? Is that you? Why aren't you at work?'

A wave of relief flooded through me. My legs shook as I entered the living room to see her sitting with Dana. They had made themselves comfortable, with a tray of tea things on the table, complete with the rest of the scones I had brought home the previous evening.

'Where's Poppy?' they chorused, looking up in surprise.

Flustered and breathless, I decided it would be tactless to explain that in my haste to check my mother wasn't being murdered, I had not stopped to collect Poppy from Jane's house.

'I thought you'd like to come with me to fetch her from Jane's house,' I said to my mother, with an embarrassed smile.

She knew I was lying.

'You forgot I was coming, didn't you?' she demanded, but she was smiling, her accusation playful rather than angry.

'Honestly, I did,' I admitted, flopping down on a chair and catching my breath. 'It completely went out of my head. There's been so much going on.' I hesitated, afraid to mention that Dana was a suspected murderer. 'What with the fair, and the police, and now Holly's not well.' To my chagrin, I burst into tears. On top of everything else, Holly's condition was affecting me more than I had realised. 'It's all so sudden. I mean, of course, Jane knows Holly's old, but still, you never expect it when it happens. And Poppy's going to be devastated,' I concluded my account of Holly's decline. 'It's not as if I can explain it to Poppy. One day, Holly just won't be there anymore.' I blew my nose, struggling to hold back more tears.

'Poppy probably understands a lot more than you give her credit for,' Dana assured me, pouring me a cup of tea. 'After all, what's happening is natural, and Poppy must have much more highly developed instincts than we do. She must sense that Holly's very old, and won't be around much longer.'

I hoped she was right. Poppy was certainly no fool, but I had heard stories of dogs dying of broken hearts when they lost their familiar companions, and I ached for Poppy more than for Jane. At least Jane understood what was going to happen and had time to prepare herself for the inevitable loss.

'She just has to get back in the saddle,' my mother said firmly, with her usual practicality.

As usual, my mother's approach to someone else's suffering seemed to show a complete lack of empathy. This time, what she said didn't even make sense.

'Who has to get back in the saddle?' I asked.

'Jane, of course. She needs to find herself another dog. That'll sort her out,' she said briskly.

'Oh mother,' I sighed. 'It's not that simple.'

But there was no point in trying to explain that another dog would never replace Holly who had been Jane's constant companion for over twelve years. She had seen Jane through the loss of her husband, and that kind of relationship was irreplaceable.

My mother frowned. 'I take it Jane had another dog before Holly?'

'Yes, I think so.'

'There you are then,' my mother said, as though she had won an argument.

'Mum,' I protested, nearly laughing with exasperation at her lack of understanding. 'You're missing the point.'

'I think you're the one who's missing the point,' she replied tartly.

In the end, we agreed to differ, and we set off to collect Poppy, leaving Dana to clear away the tea things.

'You go and get Poppy,' she insisted. 'I'll deal with this. It won't take me a minute.'

'Dana seems very nice, but she has an air of sadness,' my mother said as we set off down the lane. 'She insisted on sleeping on the couch tonight so I can have the spare bed. And she changed the sheets. That's nice of her, isn't it? So, how did you two meet? I hope your taking in a lodger doesn't mean you're struggling financially?'

Uncertain how much to disclose, I hesitated. My mother was bound to hear people talking about the murder at the fair, and it was no secret that Dana had been questioned by the police in connection with it. With luck, my mother might not learn that Dana was suspected of having committed the murder herself. It all depended on the discretion of everyone who spoke to my mother. Given there was a good chance my mother was going to hear a melodramatic version of recent events from someone like Maud, I decided it would be better for me to come clean and tell her everything myself, before anyone else could describe Dana as a dangerous psychopath. To cap it all, I wasn't sure how much Dana herself had already shared with my mother. With my mind going round in circles about what to say, I walked on in silence for a few minutes, trying to decide how to answer her.

The sun was fairly low in the sky but it was still a few hours until nightfall, and the air was warm. A light breeze fluttered the leaves on the trees, doing nothing to lower the temperature. After the heat of the day, it was a perfect evening, but I was too stressed to enjoy the walk.

'There's clearly something on your mind,' my mother said at last. 'You know if you're struggling, we can help you out. We're not loaded, but we have a little put by, and we're not going to sit back and watch while you get yourself into hot water. Whatever you do, I want you to promise that you'll speak to us before you start taking out any loans. It's all too easy to panic and do something without thinking that only makes the situation a hundred times worse than it needs to be.'

For a moment, I assumed she was worried about my friendship with Dana. Realising she was talking about money, I smiled. Thanking her for her generosity, I assured her my finances were in reasonable shape. My wages were low, but they were enough to cover my daily needs. If I wasn't able to save, at least Rosecroft was mine, a mortgage-free nest egg for my old age, should I need it. Thanks to my great aunt's generosity, my situation was secure, which was more than could be said for many people.

'What is it then?' she pressed me. 'It can't just be about Holly. She's a dog, for goodness' sake, and she's not even yours.'

Never having owned a pet, my mother had no idea how callous her statement sounded to a dog lover. Hoping she wouldn't be so insensitive in front of Jane, I shook my head, wishing that we had more in common. She was my mother, and we loved each other, but this wasn't the first time we had struggled to understand one another's viewpoint. My mother liked to see herself as slightly wild and rebellious, but she was actually very conventional and very old fashioned in her outlook. She had finally accepted that I was content with my independent lifestyle, but my status as a single woman still held a faint stigma of spinsterhood in her mind. She was convinced I would never be happy until I was married with at least one child under my belt. For my mother, work and dogs counted for nothing, because she herself had never pursued a career or owned a pet. It was depressing to see how narrow-minded she was. It had taken me a long time to understand that her attitude was an expression of her insecurity about her own life. Despite our differences, we generally got on very well, but I wasn't sure how she would react if she discovered her daughter had opened her home to a suspected murderer. I wasn't even sure how to justify my decision myself. I dreaded hearing her reaction and could just imagine what she would say.

You invited a murderer into your home? Seriously, Emily, that's unbelievable. What on earth were you thinking? She has to go. Right now. You really are a naïve fool to let her sleep under your roof.

And how would I respond?

Rosecroft is my home. You can't dictate what I can and can't do in my own home. Or would I concede that my invitation to Dana had been a mistake?

'Well?' she insisted.

Tentatively, I enquired how much she knew about Dana.

She considered. 'Apart from the fact that she used to work for the local newspaper after she left the fair, and the police have accused her of murdering her ex's new girlfriend, not a lot. What's the matter now? You look as if you've seen a ghost. Do shut your mouth before an insect flies in and chokes you. Really, Emily, what *is* the matter with you today? This can't all be about you forgetting my visit, although how you could do that is a mystery to me, but there it is. You always were absent-minded. Now I insist you tell me what's wrong? You're not ill, are you?'

'No, no, I'm not ill. I'm absolutely fine. And it's really lovely to see you.'

She yelped in amazement as I flung my arms around her and gave her a hug.

'Well, well, that was very nice, I must say, if a little belated. Now, let's go and get Poppy. It's not like you to forget about her, but I suppose you were all in a tizzy when you realised what you'd done. I don't understand how you can be so reckless.'

'I thought you were okay with her staying?'

'What are you talking about?'

For a few moments we talked at cross purposes until it became obvious that I thought my mother was talking about Dana staying at Rosecroft, while she was referring to my oversight in forgetting about her visit. Still annoyed with myself, I could only apologise. Thankfully my mother was far more forgiving than a lot of other people might have been. She was certainly more open-minded than I had ever given her credit for.

'Sometimes you really surprise me,' I told her. 'In a good way.'

'You're not always very adept at judging people's characters,' she replied, in a veiled reference to my disastrous history with boyfriends. 'Speaking of which,' she added, with a sudden gleam in her eyes, 'what's happened to Barry?'

She looked dashed on hearing that he had a girlfriend. 'Never mind,' she said, patting my arm. 'It probably won't last.'

I didn't confess that I hoped she was right, instead murmuring that they seemed to be well suited.

'Yes, well, appearances can be deceptive, as we both know.'

Excited to see us, Poppy ran straight over to my mother. I smiled to see how pleased she was to be greeted first; Poppy certainly knew how to charm people. Holly was asleep and we could see that Jane had been crying. Before we left, Poppy ran over to her aged friend and nudged her head but Holly did not respond. We weren't sure if she was still alive, but Poppy persevered, whimpering and growling gently, until the old dog finally opened her eyes briefly and jiggled her tail. We were all pleased to see her respond to Poppy's pestering, but I couldn't help thinking it looked as though she might be saying goodbye. With a lump in my throat, I listened as Jane told us Hannah and Adam had agreed to help her take Holly to the vet the next day. We hugged Jane and said goodbye and set off home, trying not to feel too downhearted but it was hard, even though we knew Holly had lived a happy life filled with love. Poppy was subdued on the way home, and I wondered how much she understood. That evening we were a sombre household. Poppy lay at my feet all evening without once agitating to go outside, as if she wanted to reassure me that she would never leave me, something I found too painful to contemplate. Dana made supper and we ate mostly in silence, each of us preoccupied with our own thoughts.

'Jane needs to get another dog as soon as she can,' my mother repeated as we were clearing away the supper things.

Holly was alive and might recover and stay with Jane for another year, or possibly even longer. It seemed premature to start looking for her replacement, and I said as much, quite crossly.

'I'm not suggesting she gets another dog as a substitute for Holly,' my mother replied. 'This has nothing to do with Holly's advanced age, or her health issues, or whatever her problem is. I just think it would be a good idea for Jane to think about giving a home to another dog. It would be company for Holly, as well as helping Jane when Holly dies. There are plenty of rescue dogs waiting for someone to give them a loving home.'

What my mother was saying made sense. The following morning I left Poppy at Rosecroft with my mother and Dana, who seemed to be getting on well. On and off throughout the day, Hannah and I discussed Jane's sad situation and my mother's solution. As it happened, a cockapoo in the village had whelped a couple of months earlier, and the puppies were technically old enough to be separated from their mother, so Hannah suggested we go and check them out. Since Poppy had been living with me for nearly three years, my friend seemed to regard me as some kind of canine expert. That made me laugh, but I agreed to go with her anyway, after my mother left. The next day, Hannah came to work looking sombre. In the vet's opinion, Holly was suffering, and the kindest option had been to put Holly to sleep as there was no chance she would recover. Basically, she was dying of old age.

The following morning I went into work late after seeing my mother off at the bus stop. Poppy was at home with Dana, and when we closed at the end of the day Hannah persuaded me to go with her to investigate the litter of new puppies she had heard about. The dog breeder lived a short bus ride from the village and we found the house easily. A young woman opened the door and smiled in welcome when she heard who we were.

'Hannah,' she said. 'You called earlier, didn't you? About a puppy for your mother? We still have one available. Come on in and see her. They're in here.'

She led us into a cosy kitchen, where a white dam lay stretched out on a grey dog bed looking half asleep, while a wriggling group of puppies jostled each other beside her. Hannah exclaimed that the mother was beautiful, and the cockapoo puppies were all adorable. She was right. Their owner told us that all the puppies had been taken apart from one, whom she told us was the cutest of them all. Apparently prospective buyers had been put off because she was smaller than the others in the litter, although the breeder assured us she was perfectly healthy.

'We'll take her,' Hannah said at once. 'When can we come and fetch her?'

The breeder hesitated. 'Doesn't your mother want to see her before making up her mind? Choosing a dog is a very personal thing. She'll want to make sure this is the right dog for her. I can't just hand a puppy over if I'm not sure she'll be going to a suitable home.'

'It's okay,' Hannah assured her. 'My mother's always had dogs. She knows how to take care of them.'

The breeder nodded and told us she knew Jane and Holly. She was sorry to learn about Holly, but was still reluctant to commit to selling the remaining puppy until Jane had met her.

'I really would like Jane to come and see the puppy for herself,' she insisted. 'From what you've told me, it might be too early. She possibly needs more time to come to terms with losing Holly before she takes in a new dog.'

'Don't worry,' Hannah replied, picking up the tiny creature that had not yet found a new home. 'My mother's bound to love this little one.'

The puppy wriggled and squeaked. She had beautiful huge black eyes and a shiny black nose, and her legs and body were covered in light grey fur. Hannah was right when she said the smallest puppy in the litter was adorable.

'We'll definitely take her,' Hannah said. 'My mother's going to fall in love with her at first sight. Who wouldn't?'

I waited until we were back in Ashton Mead before voicing my misgivings. Hannah had just promised her mother would want the little puppy, before Jane had even set eyes on her.

'Don't worry,' Hannah repeated. 'We'll just tell my mum that no one wanted the smallest one in the litter. Once she sees her, she'll thank us. Trust me.'

Although I couldn't imagine anyone not falling for the tiny puppy, as the breeder had said, choosing a dog was a very personal matter.

'You didn't choose Poppy,' Hannah pointed out.

She was right. Poppy had been foisted on me, left to me in my great aunt's will as part of the bequest that included Rosecroft. Under the terms of the will, if I had refused the dog, I would have forfeited the cottage.

'I hadn't just lost another dog,' I pointed out.

'That's all the more reason why my mother will want that little puppy,' Hannah assured me. 'You're just miffed because your mother's right.'

8

POPPY FLUNG HERSELF AT me with her usual exuberance as soon as I walked through the door. Barking for my attention, she rolled over onto her back for a tummy rub as soon as I started petting her. Dana assured me she had been no trouble while Hannah and I had been out at work and visiting the dog breeder. The weather had been fine and she had spent all day in the garden, alternately patrolling the fences for foxes and dozing in the shade.

'How did it go?' Dana wanted to know.

I told her how keen Hannah had been to secure the remaining puppy for her mother.

Dana laughed. 'It sounds as though Hannah would like that puppy herself.'

The three of us had settled down together, but I could not afford to continue supporting Dana financially indefinitely. Claiming to be worried the police had not yet finished with her, she had delayed starting to look for work. In the meantime, a couple of days passed without any police attention. Hoping they had accepted that she was innocent, we began to discuss what job she might look for.

'I don't want to do just anything,' she said earnestly.

Thinking about her rent-free room, I almost gave a sharp retort, but thought better of it. Being a suspect in a murder enquiry was not easy, as I knew from painful experience, and I didn't want to seem unsympathetic. The weather was warm and Poppy's fur must have been uncomfortable. She didn't like going to the dog grooming parlour, even though we had been to one in Swindon where the staff were lovely. Given the time it took to reach the groomers, and Poppy's reluctance to go there, I had bought a set of clippers which I had already used several times to trim her fur, with varying degrees of success. With Dana holding her, the operation was much easier and quicker than when I had tried to do it on my own, and it didn't take very long to trim the fur on her body and legs. Nervous about using the clippers close to her eyes, I didn't touch the curly fur on her head. This gave the illusion that her head was proportionally bigger than her body, which somehow made her look even more cute than usual.

That night Poppy seemed restless when we went to bed. She refused to settle, but prowled from room to room, growling. Thinking she needed to go outside, I climbed out of bed, pulled on jeans and a shirt over my nightie, and went downstairs. Poppy trotted after me but once we reached the hall and I had put my shoes on, she refused to leave the house and barked frantically when I opened the front door.

'It's all right,' I assured her. 'There's no one out there.'

But she continued to pull me away from the door. Annoyed with her for dragging me out of bed for nothing, I stomped back to my room, tore off my jeans and shirt and fell into bed. Eventually I drifted back to sleep, until something woke me at three in the morning.

For a few seconds I nestled under my duvet, still half in a dream. Poppy started barking frantically so I clambered groggily out of bed to see what she wanted. It was unusual for her to disturb me in the night, and this was the second time she had woken me up. I hoped she wasn't ill. Intending to take her out in the back garden, I didn't bother to put any clothes on over my pyjamas. Reaching the foot of the stairs, I noticed a draught coming from the living room. As I walked towards the open door of the room, Poppy whimpered and hung back. It was a moment before I understood what had happened. With a cry of alarm, I snatched Poppy up before she could risk injuring herself. I ran back to the hall and thrust my feet into my trainers, without stopping to tie the laces. Poppy continued barking furiously but she made no attempt to wriggle out of my arms, as though she realised it could be dangerous. Hurrying back into the front room, I switched on the light before pulling back the curtain to reveal a jagged hole in the window. Glittering shards littered the floor and the curtain was speckled with splinters of glass.

My initial reaction was one of relief that my mother was not there when it happened. Not only would she have been frightened, but she would have seized on the opportunity to criticise my lifestyle. Somehow she would have been convinced that no one would have dared to break my front window if I was living with a man. My relief was quickly superseded by fury, because Poppy could have been seriously injured by some vandal's thoughtless attack on my property. Shutting the living room door so that Poppy could not go in there, I changed my shoes in case there were specks of glass caught underneath my trainers, before going to the kitchen. Poppy jumped out of my arms and I was putting the kettle on when Dana joined me. I could tell at once she had seen what had happened in the living room. She stared at me, aghast, her face ashen in the bright kitchen light. In a trembling voice she asked me if I was all right. I nodded, fighting back tears of rage.

'Who could've done it?' I stammered when I found my voice. 'I know some of the villagers disapprove of my taking you in, but I can't believe anyone would do something so dangerous. What if Poppy had gone in there before me? She could have been seriously injured. It doesn't bear thinking about. It's so horrible.'

Poppy looked up at me and wagged her tail as though to reassure me she was unhurt.

'You don't know it was someone from the village,' Dana pointed out. 'And you don't know it was directed specifically at you. What I mean is, it could've been someone from the fairground. They know I'm staying here and no doubt plenty of them are ready to believe the lies being spread about me. To be honest, I've got a pretty good idea who it was,' she added darkly.

After a mug of tea, we went into the living room to assess the damage. It was fortunate the curtain had been closed as it had caught most of the broken glass, but it was going to be almost impossible to remove all of the splinters from the heavy fabric. It was an old curtain, one that I had inherited along with the cottage, and I decided the only sensible course would be to get rid of it. It was dusty and faded, and I had been intending to replace it one day, when I could afford it. New curtains were expensive. The carpet would have to be thoroughly hoovered and then carefully checked for fragments of glass. We went back to bed but I didn't go back to sleep and doubted whether Dana did either. Even with Poppy to alert us to any further trouble, it was uncomfortable lying in bed upstairs, knowing there was a broken window on the ground floor where someone might climb in. I was relieved when the night was over.

The next morning, Dana fiercely opposed the suggestion that we involve the police, and she convinced me there was no point in reporting the incident. Nothing had been stolen and no one had come into the house. Poppy would have barked if they had. So it was highly unlikely the police would find any evidence to help them trace the culprit, if they even conducted a search. With a murder to investigate, they were hardly likely to pay much attention to a report about a broken window. That was the only real damage, and it was not worth making an insurance claim for the repair. Dana offered to organise a carpet cleaner and a replacement window while I was at work, and so it was settled. Since I was nervous about leaving Poppy at Rosecroft, in case she trod on broken glass, I called Jane quite early to ask if she would have Poppy for the day and she was happy to agree.

Jane smiled when she saw us. 'Poppy looks adorable with her fur trimmed,' she said. No longer looking as forlorn as when she had first lost Holly, she invited me in with a cheery smile. 'Come and meet Lily properly,' she said, referring to her new puppy. 'Hopefully Poppy will be a good influence on her,' she added as we went indoors. 'I've started training her, but we've got a way to go. At the moment, she doesn't seem to have much of a clue.' She laughed. 'She's a clever little thing, and very keen to please, so she won't be much trouble to train, but she's too young to have much control yet, and she is still very little, although she's grown even in the few days she's been here, and that has to mean she feels comfortable with me. I suspect the rest of the litter barged her out of the way when they wanted to feed. She's still tiny but she's going to catch up fast.'

With Jane chatting contentedly about her new puppy, I had to acknowledge Hannah's good sense in acquiring a puppy for her mother so soon after Holly died. Lily was a fetching little bundle of fluff. Once a lively puppy who had been a source of irritation to her old companion, Holly, Poppy had grown into a calm adult who ignored the high spirited puppy yapping and squealing for her attention. Jane and I laughed at Lily's antics as she pestered Poppy. My broken window no longer felt as traumatic as it had seemed in the middle of the night. When I told Jane briefly what had happened, she suggested it had been kids, messing around, rather than a deliberate attack on Rosecroft. I hoped she was right.

Hannah was shocked when I told her what had happened. She was adamant I should have contacted the police about the damage to my property straightaway. According to her, valuable time had been lost by leaving it so long without reporting the incident. But we both knew there was nothing really to be done. Even if I had called the police as soon as I discovered the broken window, the vandals would have been long gone by the time the police arrived, however swiftly they responded to my call. Still, it was too late to rectify that now.

'I said you were asking for trouble, inviting Dana to live with you,' Hannah said brusquely.

When I pointed out we didn't know whether the broken window had anything to do with my new tenant, she scoffed and asked me if I really thought it was a coincidence, my window being smashed so soon after Dana moved in. I insisted that it was impossible to say why it had happened.

'Exactly,' she retorted. 'That's my point. You don't know if it happened because Dana's moved in with you. So seeing as you don't know, you have to be sensible and act accordingly.'

'What are you talking about?'

'You know what I mean. You have to ask Dana to leave. Her presence is putting you at risk. What if it turns out she had something to do with what happened? You're sticking your neck out for a woman who might have committed murder. Think about it. Is your decision sensible? Is it fair on Poppy? It's bad enough you wanting to offer a home to a suspected psychopath, but now you've got some unidentified enemy out to get you as well. This has to stop before you get hurt.'

But I remained adamant that I trusted Dana and believed she was innocent, and I had never been one to give in to bullies. Angrily I reminded Hannah how I had stood by her when she had been suspected of murdering her business rival.

'I would have thought that you of all people would be more sympathetic to Dana's plight,' I told her crossly.

'This is different, and you know it.'

'How is it any different? I believed you were innocent and I believe Dana is too.'

'The difference is that firstly you hardly know her, and secondly my troubles never put you in personal danger. So if you don't go to the police, I will.' She glared at me.

'You can say what you like to whoever you like,' I replied. 'But if you tell the police my window was broken in a deliberate attack on Rosecroft, I'll deny it. I'll say you are overdramatising a trivial accident.'

'It's not trivial if you could have been hurt,' she insisted. 'Or Poppy. How would you feel if she'd been injured?'

'Well, she wasn't, so just drop it, will you? This isn't your problem. You're as bad as my mother trying to manipulate me into doing what *you* want.'

I was pleased when a group of customers entered the tea shop and we had no time to continue our argument. Lily was fast asleep when I picked Poppy up, but Jane assured me the two dogs seemed to coexist quite happily, and she hoped they would start playing with one another before too long. Back at home, I was pleased that my old curtains had gone and the carpet looked spotless, and astonished that the broken window had already been replaced. All that remained was to find some suitable secondhand curtains, and the room would be back to normal.

'I can't believe you got all that done so quickly,' I told Dana.

She smiled. 'As a woman in journalism you learn to be resilient.'

I had been thinking about that. 'You worked as an investigative reporter,' I said. 'Can't you look into what happened here and find out who's responsible?'

Dana shook her head. 'I don't need to look into it to find out. I know who killed Paris, and I know the same person is behind the attack last night. What's more, I know this persecution won't stop until he's behind bars. I'd offer to move out, but I think it's too late for that. He's discovered you're my friend and he's going to nurse a grudge against you from now on, whether I'm here or not. I think you should have a burglar alarm installed.'

Poppy let out an indignant bark.

Dana bent down to stroke her head. 'No one who sees Poppy is going to view her as a serious deterrent.'

Poppy turned her back on Dana, but I didn't find it easy to dismiss what she had said. A shiver of fear trickled down my spine as I wondered what Dana's enemy might be planning to do next.

9

A FEW DAYS PASSED uneventfully and I was beginning to hope that the rock through my window had been a one off stray incident and best forgotten about. Despite Hannah's reservations, Dana and I continued to be friends, and nothing more was said about her moving out. I sounded Hannah out about the possibility of her giving Dana a job at the tea shop, but Hannah dismissed that idea at once. She said it was bad enough for her to continue employing a suspected murderer's landlady, but at least I had been working at the tea shop for a few years and people were used to seeing me there. If she suddenly introduced Dana as a waitress, she would almost certainly lose most if not all of her regular customers.

'It's out of the question,' she concluded. 'I'm surprised you asked me.'

I could have argued with her as a friend, but Hannah was my boss and there was a possibility that losing her goodwill might cost me my job. So I walked away, muttering that the police had stopped questioning Dana because they knew she was innocent, and it was a pity when inflexible people refused to see beyond their own mistakes.

Hearing that my window had 'accidentally' broken, and been repaired, my mother offered to buy me new curtains as an early birthday present. I was very happy to accept her generous gift, and my new curtains were now on order and due to arrive in a couple of weeks. In the meantime, Dana and I felt uncomfortable spending the evening in the living room. Although no one ever passed by outside, we felt exposed sitting in front of the unprotected window, so we decided to go to the pub where we hoped to meet up with my friends. We hadn't arranged to see them, but I expected they would be there.

Poppy seemed restless when we entered the bar, but as we had just walked from Mill Lane where we lived to the pub at the end of the High Street, I decided to ignore her whimpering to go outside. Hannah and Adam were there and they seemed happy to see us, even though Hannah and I had almost fallen out earlier on that day. She made no reference to our disagreement and greeted Dana cheerfully as we sat down. Toby was leaning on the bar chatting to his girlfriend, Michelle, who worked at the pub. I was pleased when Barry entered, but less happy to see Samantha follow him in. They went up to the bar together and stood chatting with Toby, while Michelle pulled their pints. Seated facing the bar, I took advantage of the opportunity to study Samatha surreptitiously. Had she been wearing heels, she would have been nearly as tall as Barry, who was six foot. Her hair was a mousy blonde, which I assumed was her natural colour, and she was slim without being elegant. She looked like a down to earth outdoorsy kind of girl. Barry put his arm around her and they walked across to join us. Hannah started chatting to Samantha, and I listened to their conversation. We learned that Barry's new girlfriend worked in Swindon, and she had met Barry in a café near the police station.

'I work in a recruitment agency,' she said. 'It's nothing very glamorous but I enjoy it because it involves meeting people, so no two days are exactly the same. It can be quite challenging at times, because you have to be diplomatic.'

'I can see you'd be good at that,' Hannah said. She complimented Samantha on her friendly and approachable manner and I nodded in agreement.

Hearing what Samantha did, I glanced at Dana, wondering whether Barry's girlfriend might be able to help her find a job. The atmosphere in the bar was quiet and relaxed and I was enjoying the return to normality, after the unpleasantness of my broken window. Barry sneezed, which made Poppy bark, and we all laughed.

'I think I must be allergic to something,' he muttered apologetically.

Poppy came over to me and put her head on my foot. Looking round, I saw that a group of people from the fairground had arrived and were sitting down around a table at the other end of the bar casting hostile glances at Dana who shifted her chair so that she was sitting with her back to them. For a small dog, Poppy had a surprisingly loud bark and several customers turned to glance at us, some irritated by the noise, others smiling sympathetically at me. Picking her up, I did my best to pacify her. She had just quietened down, when a man walked past our table on his way to the bar. With a shiver, I recognised Alfie. There was no time to try and hide my agitation because Poppy began barking in earnest. She could not have been more agitated if a fox had entered the pub and strolled over to the bar, waving its tail provocatively at her as it passed. Only by threatening to take her home and leave her there on her own, was I able to quieten her. She sat on my lap, growling softly, but these were not her usual purring sounds of pleasure. These were belligerent snarls directed at Alfie. Standing at the bar, he was chatting to Michelle who was smiling and nodding at him while Toby watched uneasily.

Mortified by Poppy's aggression, I leaned down and hid my face in her fur, murmuring to her to be quiet and stop embarrassing me in public. To be fair to Poppy, she was generally very well behaved. It was not clear what had upset her on this occasion. When I dared look up, I was relieved to see that no one from any other table was looking at us any more now the initial disturbance was over. Only Alfie was staring at me, with a curious glint in his eyes. My breath caught in my throat as I recalled what Dana had told me. In the soft lighting of the bar, he was even more attractive than I remembered, and I could easily believe he exerted some kind of charismatic power over young women. Tall and slender, he was leaning against the bar. But where most people might slump or slouch, he appeared graceful, as though every one of his muscles was perfectly aligned to support him standing there. Even from a distance, there was something magnetic about him. Whether it was the absolute stillness of his figure that was spellbinding, or my knowledge of his character, I found my gaze drawn to him. Evidently I was not being discreet, because Hannah nudged my arm.

'I think Emily's smitten,' she murmured with a grin.

'What?'

She gave me a knowing look. 'Don't give me that innocent, butter wouldn't melt in my mouth, expression.

You can't take your eyes off him. I can't say I blame you.' She giggled. 'He's lush. If I was single… ' She winked at me.

To my chagrin, I felt my cheeks turn warm with irritation. No doubt Hannah would misinterpret my blushes, but I didn't know how to disabuse her without betraying Dana's confidence.

'You've got it all wrong,' I muttered, disconcerted, but Hannah just smirked knowingly.

'He can't take his eyes off you,' she whispered.

Dana stood up abruptly and said she was leaving. Aware of Alfie's scrutiny, I was feeling increasingly uncomfortable and, with Poppy being disruptive, I decided to leave too. Dana's departure gave me the perfect opportunity to go.

'I'll come with you,' I called after her.

On the way home, Dana started telling me more about Alfie. In my turn, I told her how he had invited me onto the carousel, and a young blonde woman had come along and addressed him as 'Alfie'. Hesitantly, I described her bruises and my suspicion that someone had mistreated her.

'She looked very young,' I added.

Dana grunted. 'I expect that was Paris, the girl who was murdered.'

I was shocked, even though I had already suspected as much.

'That sounds just like Alfie. I told you, he's a psychopath.' She shuddered. 'He would have done the same to me, if I hadn't managed to get away. He's twisted, and he twists everything around him. He convinced everyone he dumped me, so they're bound to dismiss anything I say as spiteful allegations from a jilted ex.'

'What happened when you walked out on him?'

She hesitated. 'What happened was that I just couldn't take it anymore. Leaving the fair altogether was the only way I could get away from him. Alfie took it very badly. I told you he'd been planning to take over from my dad, didn't I? Well, he thought marrying me would be his ticket to stepping into my father's shoes. He thought he'd be the obvious successor once he'd persuaded my father to retire, and tried to get me to help him convince my father to move aside for a younger man. He'd always been abusive towards me, but he became really violent when he realised I wasn't prepared to fit in with his plan. Basically, he can't cope with not getting his own way. When he broke my arm and threatened to kill me, I knew he was serious. That was when I realised my life was in danger. I had to get away if I was going to survive.'

'You should've gone to the police.'

'I know, but I was young and scared, so I ran.'

'Why didn't anyone at the fair help you? You had parents, and you must have had friends there.'

'It wasn't quite like that. Alfie's a very dominant personality and he knows how to manipulate people. He persuaded me to pretend I had a series of accidents. I think some people suspected what was going on, but I was complicit in covering up Alfie's violence. In any case, what proof did I have? A hysterical young girl accusing a clever older man of beating her up. Once he persuaded me to start lying to cover up for his abuse, he would have run rings around me if I'd tried to cause trouble for him. And I was desperately afraid of having another "accident", like the one that happened to Paris. I think some people knew why I was leaving and they didn't blame me. My mother encouraged me to go.'

I confessed that I too had been the victim of a man who was, basically, a manipulative narcissist who had pursued me solely in order to get his hands on my house. I had been completely taken in by him. His protestations of love were a complete tissue of lies. He had been motivated only by money. If I hadn't discovered his secret plot to sell Poppy, I might never have seen through him.

'So Poppy saved you,' Dana said. She sighed. 'I wish I'd had her with me when Alfie was assaulting me. Although I don't suppose she would have been able to help me. She would only have got herself killed.'

Poppy stopped sniffing some weeds and looked up at Dana, her tongue hanging out of her mouth.

'It's all right, Poppy,' I said. 'No one's going to hurt you.'

'Of course, they're not,' Dana agreed. 'We're just talking.'

Poppy turned away to sniff the ground again and we walked on for a few moments in silence.

'I'm convinced Alfie killed Paris,' Dana said at last, through clenched teeth.

'Surely you can't be the only one who suspects him?' I replied. 'Other people must be aware of his violent temper, and see his girlfriends' bruises.'

'He's a psychopath. I think there's a faction among the showpeople who would like to see the back of him, but they're scared of him and worried about the backlash if the public learned there was a murderer at the fair. Can you imagine what it would do to the reputation of the fairground workers?'

'But there are bad apples everywhere,' I protested. 'And they can't cover up for a killer.'

She nodded. 'You're right, of course, but try telling them that. After centuries of suspicion and persecution, they're scared of the outcry if they hand him over to the police, and he plays on that. So they don't dare tell the police what they know, or at least suspect. But even if someone wanted to expose him, he's too clever to leave any proof, and the girls he beats up are in thrall to him and refuse to come out and tell the truth about him. It's not for nothing that he selects girls who are young and lacking in confidence. If anyone tried to cause trouble for him, the chances are it would rebound on his accuser. Look what happened to me. No one dares take that risk.'

'But you could,' I pointed out. 'And you know better than anyone how vicious he is.'

She shook her head. 'I'm not sure you fully grasp the situation. Yes, I could go to the police, but you're completely misguided if you think for one minute they'd believe me.'

'Why not? Surely the rest of the community would back you up if you spoke out?'

'Have you heard of omertà? The code of silence?'

'It sounds like the Mafia!' I cried out.

Dana scoffed. 'The Mafia only started in the mid-19th century in Sicily. Fairs have been around for centuries, although no one outside our itinerant community seems to know our history. It's shocking how ignorant most people are, and the greater their ignorance, the quicker they are to judge.'

A little shamefaced, I admitted my own ignorance of the history of the men and women who worked at the fairs. By now we had reached the lane, and we fell silent as we approached Rosecroft. I wondered if, like me, Dana was worried that we might find the cottage had been vandalised again. All was well and Poppy was soon out in the back garden on self-imposed sentry duty. As long as there were no foxes around, she was content to lie on the grass sniffing the scents carried on the night air, sometimes stirring herself to trot around the garden to hunt for insects or follow fox and squirrel tracks.

'You were going to tell me about the history of the people who work on the fairs,' I reminded Dana when we were sitting in the kitchen with a pot of tea.

'Fairs were introduced into Britain back in Roman times,' she told me. 'They were set up to facilitate trading and played a growing role in the economy of the country, especially after the Normans granted charters giving fairs legal status. By the Middle Ages, there were several thousand fairs, attracting merchants and wealth from all over Europe. Anyway, over the centuries shopping habits changed, along with everything else, and fairs started to focus more on entertainment than trading. Shows became the main attraction until the nineteenth century when steam power revolutionised rides. But fairs were groundbreaking in so many ways. A lot of rural communities only saw electric lighting for the first time at travelling fairs.'

She paused and I made appropriate noises to express my amazement at what she was telling me.

'So you see, travelling showpeople have a long and respectable history, despite what the general public think of us,' she concluded. 'Most people think of fairs as nothing more than a day of fun and thrills, but there's a lot more to our history than that.'

'I had no idea fairs played such a key role in history,' I admitted, and she smiled.

10

HANNAH WAS DISTANT WITH me the next day. As it happened, we were very busy as it was a beautiful summer's day and we were overrun with visitors to our picturesque village. When I went to the shop for some milk, the High Street was packed with tourists. From what I could see and hear, they were a mixture of Japanese, American and English. Many of them enthused over what they described as our 'quaint' village shops, and the historic bridge which allegedly dated back to Roman times. My next-door neighbour and good friend, Richard, was a historian who specialised in architecture. Before he retired, he had been a university professor of history, and was reputed to be an expert on Roman architecture, at least according to his son, Adam. Richard had assured us the bridge was not as old as the guidebooks claimed. In his opinion, there had probably been an earlier bridge across the river at the site of the existing one, which he judged to be no more than a century old. Since part of the village's attraction for visitors was the ancient bridge mentioned in literature about Ashton Mead, no one paid any attention to Richard, and guidebooks continued to be printed urging visitors to view the fine example of an early Roman bridge.

Despite my financial misgivings, there were definite benefits to having Dana staying with me. Without a word being exchanged, she had taken over doing the laundry, I no longer had to stack or empty the dishwasher and we never ran out of milk or tea. She would have liked me to leave Poppy with her during the day, but Jane was insistent that she wanted Lily to spend time with another dog and I suspected she enjoyed Poppy's company as much as Lily did. My loyalty was to Jane before Dana who, after all, had only been my friend for a short time. In any case, living at Rosecroft rent free, Dana was in no position to make any demands on me.

Apart from indulging Jane's wishes, I liked collecting Poppy from Jane's house. Lily had only been with Jane for a few weeks, but she had already grown and put on some weight. She had a funny little way of barking, throwing her head back and letting out a squeaky howl that made us laugh. When I imitated Lily's high-pitched bark, she answered with one of her own, and our exchanges had Jane in hysterics. Lily really was very cute, with big eyes and long ears framing her little face, and it was lovely to see her comforting Jane in her loss. Holly had been with her for a long time, and Jane's voice still shook slightly when she mentioned her old dog, but she seemed content. Her house was a positive environment for Poppy who tolerated Lily's playful pestering and occasionally deigned to chase her across the garden. It was very one-sided as Poppy was fast and would overtake the puppy almost at once, running off and returning, as though to find out what was keeping Lily. Their game encouraged the puppy to run around, and they both seemed to enjoy themselves. Jane was confident that, as Lily grew, she would become a more suitable playmate for Poppy who liked to run around, chasing and being chased.

'It's good for both of them to be outside running around,' Jane told me, and I agreed. 'I keep them in at the hottest part of the day,' she added, but there was no need for her to reassure me that she was looking after Poppy well. She was more experienced with looking after dogs than I was, and I could leave Poppy with her, confident my little companion was in safe hands.

Enjoying a very short lull between lunch and tea, Hannah and I sat down together with a pot of tea. I was really pleased to hear she wanted to spend more time with me.

'I thought you were annoyed with me,' I told her, and immediately regretted my words. 'Anyway, it's fun seeing Lily. You were right to insist on getting her for your mother, by the way. She's perfect.'

'Why would I be annoyed with you?' she asked.

I didn't want to point out that Hannah had been unusually short tempered with me since Dana had moved in with me, or to confess that Dana had suggested Hannah might be put out that I had found a new friend, so I just shrugged. Before she could press me to explain, a group of Japanese tourists surged into the tea shop, chattering excitedly, and we were soon busy setting out trays for our customers, taking care that everything looked quintessentially English.

'We serve a traditional English tea,' I told our customers and they all took out their phones and cameras to take pictures of Hannah's scones and pretty tea cups.

After that, we were busy for the remainder of the afternoon, and had no more time to chat. We were late closing and despite our earlier agreement that we would spend more time together, we barely had time to clear up before I was due to leave to collect Poppy from Jane's. It had been a lovely day, with only a short shower in the early afternoon to cool the air slightly, so the two dogs had probably spent a lot of time in the garden, and I was keen to see they were getting on together.

On my way to Jane's house, I was startled to see Alfie walking towards me across the green. I didn't want to talk to him, but he hailed me and hurried across the grass to join me. It was impossible to ignore him, so I stopped. He really was very good looking. I thought of Victorian romantic heroines who would swoon on seeing the hero, and felt slightly dizzy as he gazed into my eyes and smiled. But Dana's words rang in my head, warning me that he was a dangerous psychopath.

'You live in the village, don't you?' he asked.

Flustered, I nodded, wondering what he wanted with me.

'I saw you in the pub the other night,' he went on.

I nodded again, keeping my eyes fixed on the ground.

'You were with Dana,' he added. 'What's your name?'

I hesitated for only a second. He could easily find out by asking almost anyone in the village. Afraid of provoking his temper by seeming openly hostile, I forced a smile as I told him my name.

'Emily,' he repeated. 'That's a beautiful name. It suits you.'

'I need to hurry,' I blurted out. 'Some people are expecting me and I don't want to keep them waiting.' I didn't explain that the 'people' were actually one woman, a small dog and a puppy, none of whom would mind if I was late.

Alfie took a step closer, watching me speculatively, his eyes sparkling mischievously. 'I'm Alfie. I just want to know what that bitch has been saying about me,' he muttered.

'I don't know what you mean.'

'Dana. What's she said about me?'

'What makes you think she's been talking about you?' I retorted, annoyed at his presumption that I would confide in him. 'She's never mentioned you to me.'

Actually, we had been discussing him quite a lot, but I wasn't about to tell him that. Dana was my friend, and my loyalty lay with her. Alfie was a stranger to me and, from everything Dana had said about him, he was hardly someone I wanted to get to know.

He shrugged. 'Just as long as she's not been spreading her filthy lies about me,' he said. 'You can't believe a word that comes out of her mouth. She's had it in for me ever since I dumped her.'

Hoping he wouldn't offer to walk with me, I repeated that people were waiting for me.

'Where's your cute little dog?' he asked. 'I hope nothing's happened to her. You need to watch her. Dogs can run off and disappear when you least expect it.'

Terrified that his words were a threat, I turned away, but he reached out and grabbed my elbow. Startled by the strength of his grip, I waited anxiously to hear what he had to say. His next words made me tremble.

'Be wary of Dana,' he murmured urgently, his eyes boring into mine. 'She's a very dangerous woman. Don't say anything that might provoke her. I'd hate to see you get hurt.'

With that, he turned and strode away, leaving me to make my way to Jane's house alone.

As always, Poppy was happy to see me, and I was almost overcome with relief on seeing her safe and well. Lily seemed excited by my arrival too, and they both jumped up, eager for attention. I wanted to make a fuss of Lily and get to know her, without putting Poppy's nose out of joint, and spent a few minutes sitting on the floor petting them both.

'It's just as well I've got two hands,' I laughed.

Next to Poppy, Lily looked tiny. She was very sweet and it was lovely to observe Jane watching her adoringly. When I clambered to my feet, Jane picked Lily up and cuddled her, talking softly to her, telling her that Poppy would be back to play with her again the next day. As though she understood, Poppy wagged her tail. Leaving Jane cleaning the carpet where Lily had done a little wee in her excitement, I took Poppy home. I looked out for Alfie as we went, but didn't see him. We hurried past the caravans and trailers that were still parked down near the river. Poppy whimpered as we approached and tried to pull me away, but I kept going towards Mill Lane and home. As we were about to turn towards Rosecroft, I heard someone calling my name. I spun round and saw Alfie peering out between two trailers.

'I thought it was you,' he said, advancing towards me with a smile. 'I was hoping to see you again.'

Apprehensively, I watched him approach. Poppy crouched down at my feet, growling softly at Alfie, who glanced down at her and laughed. Not fazed by her hostility, he reached down to pat her head to assert his dominance, but Poppy was having none of it. She barked and flicked her head to one side, snapping at him. Alfie snatched his hand away. Just for a second, an ugly expression crossed his face, and I was afraid he was going to hit her. To my relief, he recovered his equanimity quickly, while I apologised for Poppy's aggression.

'It's not like her,' I assured him. 'She's usually very friendly. She just gets nervous around strangers, but she's harmless.' I wondered if that had been a sensible admission. It might have been safer for Poppy if Alfie had been wary of approaching her.

Alfie shrugged and brushed the incident off as though it was unimportant. 'She's feisty, that's all,' he said. 'It's easy to look after a dog that's naturally submissive. Dogs with personality like this one or more of a challenge, but they can be trained to obey. You just have to let them know who's boss.'

He laughed again, and I joined in uneasily, relieved that the immediate threat had passed. Poppy turned to stare at me, seemingly perplexed by my amusement.

'It's all right,' I told her, 'Alfie knows you don't mean any harm. She's just not used to you,' I explained, turning back to Alfie. 'She's very possessive with me,' I added.

Poppy turned her back on me and began sniffing the grass.

Quelling a flicker of unease, I smiled at Alfie. There was no doubt that Poppy was an acute judge of character. Several times in the past, she had warned me against men who had turned out to be selfish narcissists. When it came to a choice between Alfie and Dana, there was no ambiguity about which of them Poppy trusted. If I followed her instincts, I would turn and run from Alfie and never speak to him again. But he was standing in front of me, smiling. When he invited me to his caravan, I glanced at Poppy before nodding uncertainly. In that instance, it occurred to me that if I could persuade Alfie to trust me, I might be able to coax a confession from him.

He led the way past trailers and I dragged Poppy along with me, hoping I wasn't risking both of our lives. The sensible course of action would have been to run off when he first invited me to join him, but curiosity led me on.

Struggling to keep up with him, I enquired what he had meant about Dana. 'What lies has she been spreading about you?'

He didn't answer.

'Do tell,' I added, as we came to a halt. 'I do love a bit of gossip!' I giggled and tried to flutter my eyelashes seductively at him.

Before he could reply, a young woman emerged from a nearby caravan.

'There you are,' she cried out impatiently, looking at Alfie. 'I thought you were never coming back. The tea's been brewed for ages. Must be well stewed by now.' She put her hands on her hips and glared at him. 'Well, are you coming in or not? And don't blame me if the tea's cold.'

The woman was slim and blonde and pretty, not unlike the recent murder victim.

Alfie called back to her that he was on his way. 'And that tea had better not be cold,' he added crossly.

'You've only yourself to blame if it is,' she replied, and flounced back into the trailer without giving me a second glance.

Explaining that his sister had summoned him in for tea, Alfie issued me with another warning to be careful of Dana, before he turned away. I was disappointed that he didn't invite me to join him and his sister for tea, but Poppy wagged her tail and frisked around my feet, as though a weight had lifted from her shoulders. If she could talk, I had the impression she would have told me I'd just had a lucky escape.

'And you're a jackass if you believe that woman's his sister,' her expression seemed to say.

11

FOR NO PARTICULAR REASON, I told no one about my
meeting with Alfie. It wasn't that I was deliberately
keeping it quiet, but somehow the right opportunity
never seemed to arise. Dana would have been the obvious
person to confide in, but she was often out and when
she was at home, she was busy in the kitchen. She was
a brilliant cook, and I never knew what she was going
to serve up next: Thai curry, beef casserole, marinaded
salmon, or spaghetti bolognese. She seemed to have no
one particular style of culinary expertise but dished up
an amazing variety of dishes. I was almost sorry she was
spending so much time visiting recruitment agencies and
going to interviews. Finding employment might mean
she would have to leave Ashton Mead, as there was very
little work to be had locally. Commuting from the village
might be inconvenient, depending on where she managed
to find a job. I had grown accustomed to her presence and
Poppy and my mother both liked her, which was always
a good sign.

Hannah was the other obvious person I could have
spoken to about Alfie, but somehow there never seemed
to be a suitable opportunity to tell her about my latest

encounters with him. It was easy to justify my reticence by persuading myself there was nothing really to tell. Admittedly Alfie was attractive, and he had invited me to his caravan, with all the possibilities that suggested. But whatever his intentions might be, my own aim was purely to pump him for information. Once he had been summoned by his "sister", the opportunity to question him had passed, and before long the fair was going to move on, and we would never see each other again. It was most likely impossible that I would ever discover the truth about Paris's death, but I couldn't stop thinking about it. Until the murderer was exposed, Dana would remain a suspect, at least to the villagers of Ashton Mead. I owed it to my friend to discover the truth, and if that meant questioning Alfie, that was what I would do.

I wondered how easy it might be to pretend to fancy Alfie. There was nothing to stop me leading him on. After all, I was a single woman. Part of the reason was that there were few eligible single men living in Ashton Mead, and I had probably met them all. When I had first arrived in the village, I had hoped a romantic relationship might develop between me and Toby, but that had never happened and he was now with Michelle. Barry had always been keen on me but, although I really liked him, I hadn't reciprocated his feelings until it was too late. All the local men I knew were either in relationships or old enough to be my father. The residents of the village were generally my parents' generation, or young married couples, and dating a married man was something I would never contemplate doing. Relationships were challenging enough without embarking on one that was doomed to cause suffering, if not for myself, then for someone else.

Happy though I was with Poppy, I was still sometimes lonely on my own. I enjoyed Dana's company and even though it was financially a stretch to have her living with me, I wasn't looking forward to her leaving.

The next morning in the tea shop, I broached the subject cautiously with Hannah, by complaining about the dearth of eligible men in the village.

'You ought to have given Barry a fair chance,' she pointed out, as I should have expected.

Hannah was fond of Barry. Knowing how keen he was on me, she had encouraged me to go out with him. We had had one fairly dull date, and that had been it as far as I was concerned, until he had kissed me at Christmas. Since then, I had started to view him differently but now it was too late to admit I might have written him off too quickly. I sighed, realising I had made yet another rash decision. In the meantime, I had more immediate concerns.

'I've always liked Barry,' I said cautiously, 'but I just never really fancied him. You can't force yourself to have feelings for someone. In any case, he's with Sam now so there's nothing to discuss.'

'Beggars can't be choosers,' she replied, rather sharply for her. 'But you're right. You've missed your chance. I hope you don't live to regret it.'

'I'm not a beggar,' I retorted. 'And I'm not desperate. I'm sure I could easily find someone to go out with if I really wanted to.'

'What are you complaining about then?' she replied, not unreasonably. 'You won't meet anyone new here in the village, but there's nothing stopping you from exploring online dating. Who knows? You might meet the man of your dreams.'

On almost anyone else's lips, that might have sounded like a sneer, but Hannah was too considerate to be deliberately unkind and I knew she meant well. Nevertheless, I held back from telling her that Alfie had invited me to visit him in his caravan. She was bound to jump to the wrong conclusion and pester me about him. Not only that, but if Hannah knew everything Dana had told me about Alfie, she would certainly try to stop me from seeing him, and I was determined to discover the truth about the murder.

Meanwhile, Hannah warmed to her topic. 'You're certainly not going to find someone by hanging around the tea shop grumbling that there are no eligible men in the village.'

Before I could protest that I wasn't grumbling, but merely commenting, a couple of our regular customers came in and we were soon occupied serving a stream of lunches. Hannah came with me to Jane's house after work that day. She claimed she just wanted to visit her mother, but when I replied that she was going there to see Lily, she didn't deny it and we both laughed. We walked along the High Street together, chatting about whether she and Adam were going to take a holiday before the winter, and if so, how Jane and I would cope with running the tea shop now Jane had Lily to consider.

'I know you can cope, with mum doing the baking. I'm just not sure it's fair to ask her now she's got Lily to think about. Lily's too small to be left alone for long, and mum can't bring her to work while she's still a puppy. We don't want her to have accidents in the tea shop! Can you imagine what some of the customers would say? And I'd probably lose my licence, or at least my five-star hygiene rating.'

While she was talking, I caught sight of a figure loitering in the street, and thought I recognised Alfie coming towards us. As I was on the point of saying something to Hannah, he disappeared, apparently darting up a side street to avoid being seen. Hannah hadn't noticed anything but carried on blithely talking about her plans for going on holiday with Adam.

'I'm really hoping you'll be up for it but, of course, I'll understand if you'd rather not. The other possibility would be to close for a fortnight. Other businesses do it. But the thing is, I'm reluctant to lose the revenue.'

'Maybe the summer isn't the best time to close the tea shop, with all the tourists,' I suggested. 'Why not go away in the autumn? Once the schools are back, everything's cheaper anyway, and late September can be a lovely time to go away. If you're thinking about going somewhere warm, July and August can actually be too hot.'

Discussing how long it might be before Jane was able to leave Lily alone for a few hours, and whether she might cope better if Poppy was with her, we drew level with the side street where I thought Alfie had vanished. I glanced along it, but there was no sign of him. With a sigh, I wondered whether I had been mistaken in thinking I had seen him. We reached Jane's and she insisted I stay to share a pot of tea and scones Hannah had brought with her. It was nearly seven o'clock by the time I went home, leaving Jane and Hannah waiting for Adam who was joining them for supper. Jane invited me to stay, but I knew that Dana would be expecting me at home. As we approached the village green, Poppy began looking around and growling, pulling on her lead to hurry me along. It was unlike her to want to rush off. Usually she loved sniffing the grass and had to be dragged away. Assuming she was remembering that we had seen Alfie there, I ignored her antics. I didn't notice Alfie approach until he was close enough to call my name, quite softly.

'I didn't want to startle you,' he said. Concealing my feelings, I thanked him politely for his consideration. 'I've been looking out for you,' he added, and I felt my face stretch in a nervous grin.

'I tried to warn you about Dana,' Alfie said earnestly, ignoring Poppy who was barking ferociously. 'I don't think you took me seriously. I've heard she's still staying with you?'

I nodded, wondering how he knew that, and whether it might be wise to deny my friendship with Dana. Who I chose to invite into my home was really none of his business. His concern to discover where she was living was alarming, but Alfie had other issues on his mind.

'You mustn't listen to a word she says about me,' he said, shifting from foot to foot. 'She'll try to convince you *I* assaulted *her*, when you must realise I'd never do anything like that. Look at me. Do I look like the kind of man who would attack a woman? You have to believe me when I tell you it was the other way round. I never lifted a finger against Dana, I swear it. Why would I lie to you? She was the one who was violent. She attacked another girl with a knife because she thought I was interested in her. And you don't want to ask her how her father died,' he added, lowering his voice to a conspiratorial whisper, and glancing around, as though to check no one was listening. 'Be careful not to say anything that might provoke her. She comes across as charming and completely normal, but underneath the veneer of good manners, she's a coldhearted monster. If you set her off, she's quite likely to attack you. She'd happily take a pop at you just for speaking to me. I mean she could physically attack you.'

I found that hard to believe of Dana, but said nothing, instead, letting him talk while I listened.

'You've only seen the act she puts on to the world, but believe me, behind the façade there's something seriously wrong with her. Once she loses control of herself, there's no knowing what she might do.' He lowered his voice. 'Recently Paris moved in with me. Dana must have heard about it, because she threatened Paris in a fit of jealousy.

It's hard to understand, because Dana and I parted company a long time ago, but she seems to think she owns me. I've tried telling her it's over, but I'm powerless to control what she does. I know this all sounds crazy, but that's because she *is* crazy. She threw a pan of boiling water at me once because she caught me winking at another girl. That was all it was, an innocent wink.'

'That's terrible,' I said, pretending to be appalled. If it was true, it would indeed be shocking, but I didn't believe him. 'It must have been an accident, but even so–'

'Accident?' Alfie repeated, shaking his head sadly. 'I only wish that was true. And then there's my lovely Paris. Someone throttled her before throwing her off the big wheel. That death was no accident. The only thing is, Paris didn't have any enemies. No sane person could have wished to harm her. It must have been Dana, lashing out in a fit of rage. No one else could have attacked Paris. She was an angel.'

'How did Dana's father die?' I asked gently, hoping to encourage him to talk freely, and so catch him out in a lie.

'He was poisoned,' Alfie replied promptly. 'The police decided it was an accident, but they never investigated what happened properly. They didn't care. He was just a travelling fairground worker to them. I told them she killed him, and they completely ignored me. They'd never listen to someone like me, but she poisoned him all right. Her own father.'

According to Dana, Alfie himself had probably stood to gain most from her father's death. And then there was my broken window. Unless Dana had crept downstairs and gone outside and smashed it herself, there was someone else who had violent impulses. It was hard to believe Alfie could be so duplicitous as to be capable of damaging Rosecroft, when he claimed to be worried about me. Yet it was also possible his hatred of Dana was powerful enough to override all other considerations. Even more likely, his professed liking for me was a sham. If I was uncertain whom to trust, Poppy had no such misgivings. She growled aggressively whenever Alfie was nearby.

'She's unnerved by all the strangers who've been here since the fair arrived,' I told Alfie, although he was the only who seemed to have that effect on her.

I waited for him to ask me back to his caravan, but he spun on his heel and walked away, leaving me on the green with Poppy who promptly started sniffing the ground again.

'You frightened him away,' I scolded her.

She looked up at me with such a miserable expression that I couldn't be cross with her for long. I knew she didn't trust Alfie and was trying to protect me.

'Come on, then,' I said, 'let's go home and see what Dana's cooked for us tonight.'

With an excited yap, Poppy trotted happily beside me towards Rosecroft, where Dana had made a lamb curry. She had kept back some meat for Poppy, who pestered me for scraps from my plate.

'No, Poppy,' I told her. 'This is curry and quite strong. It's not for you. Really, you wouldn't like what's on my plate. You've got your dinner. Dana gave you some meat.'

She continued to whimper so eventually I touched my finger in the sauce and held out a tiny speck of it for her to lick. She sniffed at it and turned her head away without trying it and promptly scoffed what was on her plate.

'I told you,' I said, laughing. 'I knew it was too spicy for you. It certainly wouldn't be any good for you, and I'm the one who'd have to clear up after you if it made you sick.'

The curry was sensational and Dana and I ate so much, it was touch and go whether either of us would have the energy to walk to the pub that evening. I was keen to go, in case Alfie was there, but Dana was tired. After we cleared up, we sat in the living room with a beer and I decided to challenge what she had told me.

'I bumped into Alfie today,' I said in as casual a tone as I could manage.

Looking surprised, Dana didn't reply but sat perfectly still, waiting to hear what I would say next.

'He mentioned a few things that didn't seem to make much sense.'

'Oh, I'm sure he did,' she replied bitterly. 'I told you, he never forgave me for walking out on him. He'd say anything to get back at me. Oh, it wasn't that he cared for me, he only ever used me to enhance his own position in the community. If he'd married me, he would have had a claim on my father's position. That was what he was after all along: power. I was just a means to an end.'

'But your father died?' I murmured.

'Yes, and that was my fault.'

I shivered on hearing her words, and scarcely dared ask what had happened. If Alfie's warnings were justified, I could be in danger. But Dana merely sat there looking sad, stroking Poppy.

'I went to see my father one evening and told him everything Alfie had done to me. I said I didn't want to marry Alfie,' she said at last. 'My father said he was relieved to hear it and assured me I had his full support and he would do whatever was necessary to prevent the marriage. Everyone would have listened to him. But the next morning, my father was found dead.' She paused. 'My father believed my allegations. He knew I wasn't a liar and, besides, I showed him my injuries. But Alfie got to him before my father had a chance to expose him as a vicious thug.' She looked directly at me. 'It's true, I'm afraid. Alfie followed me home and overheard me talking to my father. I will never forgive myself for what happened that night. It was my fault. I threatened Alfie, telling him what I would do if he didn't let me go.' She shook her head. 'I never suspected he would come after me and eavesdrop on my conversation with my father. Once Alfie realised my father was going to oppose the marriage, he wasted no time in killing him and seizing his position. Alfie is very persuasive. He convinced everyone that he was my father's choice as a successor, and no one dared contradict him. Alfie had too many friends in our community, people he had succeeded in charming with his lies and his bravado.'

I hesitated, but I had to know the truth. Trusting that Poppy would protect me if Dana turned on me, I cleared my throat nervously and spoke up. 'Alfie told me you threw a pan of boiling water at him.'

Dana's face flushed darkly. 'He said that?'

Suddenly, she stood up. Bracing myself for an assault, I watched her tear off her shirt to show me a scar on her arm where the skin was puckered and pink.

'This is where the boiling water was thrown,' she said. 'At me. By Alfie. The next time he lost his temper, he could have killed me. After that, there was no way I could marry him and, of course, my father agreed with me. That was why he died. It was my fault. I should never have told him about Alfie's attack. If I had just left the fair, without any fuss, my father would still be alive now. My mother guessed Alfie was abusing me, and she begged me to leave before he killed me, but my father was the one who died.'

She dropped her head in her hands and burst into tears. I put my arms around her, and she sobbed as though her heart was breaking. I wondered if this was the first time she had wept for her father's death.

'It's not your fault,' I whispered. 'None of this is your fault.'

But knowing whose fault it was, I was more determined than ever to make sure Alfie would no longer be free to ruin Dana's life. I just had to work out a plan to stop him, before the fair disappeared from Ashton Mead.

12

POPPY AND I WENT to the pub later on that evening, leaving Dana at home. Tired out by her emotional outburst, she said she wanted some time to herself to read for a while, after which she was going to have an early night. I felt awkward about leaving her on her own, having doubted her unjustly, but she assured me she was fine. It wasn't as if her scar was anything new for her, and she assured me it was no longer painful. My next-door neighbour, Richard, was in his front garden preparing to pull up some weeds, when we walked by. Poppy couldn't go past without stopping for him to pay her some attention, and he was happy to make a fuss of her. When I invited him to accompany us to the pub, he smiled and admitted he was feeling too tired to face his gardening.

'It looks lovely here,' I told him. 'Your efforts are certainly worthwhile, if you ask me. No, no, come away from there.'

Poppy was on her lead and I restrained her from entering a patch of bright orange and pink flowers before she could start digging them up.

'I expect she's interested in my zinnias because I planted them this morning.' Richard smiled at Poppy. 'The freshly turned earth must smell very enticing to a little dog.'

'She's probably looking for worms or something.'

'Weeding doesn't get any easier,' he said as we set off together. 'In fact, the older I get the harder it becomes.'

'You should ask Adam to help you,' I suggested.

Richard shook his head. 'He's got enough on his plate. He doesn't need to be saddled with my problems.'

'Perhaps I could help you,' I suggested.

Richard raised a sceptical eyebrow, and I laughed. We both knew my own garden needed a lot of work before I could spare any time to spend on my neighbour's plot. He admitted he had been thinking of finding a gardener to come once a month, to help him control the weeds and mow the grass. In the meantime, he was happy to abandon his front garden for the evening and come to the pub. He was always pleased to have an excuse to see Adam and Hannah. We strolled along companionably, chatting about how well the tea shop was doing, and laughing at Poppy's antics as she chased a butterfly and barked at a squirrel that scurried up a tree, far out of reach.

'She never gets it that squirrels can easily escape her by climbing a tree,' I laughed. 'Just like she doesn't understand that she'll never catch a bird. For such a clever dog, it's amazing how daft she can be.'

As I was speaking, Poppy halted and looked up at me, her head on one side.

'I don't think Poppy agrees that she's daft,' Richard chuckled, his blue eyes twinkling merrily, and Poppy wagged her tail.

It was a mild summer evening, and still a few hours before sunset, as we strolled through the village. The shops seemed to glow in the soft light of early evening, and a gentle breeze blew a few fallen leaves, sending them skittering across the road. Poppy strained at her lead, desperate to chase after them. Reaching the corner of the High Street, we found Hannah and Adam sitting with Barry and Samantha in the garden of The Plough. No one paid any attention to a group of fairground people seated on the far side of the garden. After more than a week the murder was no longer on everyone's lips, the death already overshadowed by the general business of life. I scanned the faces at their table furtively, but there was no sign of Alfie. Hiding my relief, I followed Richard as he made his way across the grass, with Poppy sniffing her surroundings eagerly.

With the prospect of a relaxing evening ahead, it was difficult to think about Dana's troubles. It was almost as though tragedy had not struck since the fair came to the village. Cliff kept the borders of the garden well stocked with different coloured flowers which Richard identified for us. Scarlet geraniums made a stunning display behind white and purple pansies which were interspersed with annuals, pink begonias and golden marigolds, while bright yellow and orange dahlias towered over the smaller plants. Delicate scent from various flowers permeated the air as we passed, a subtle fragrance that seemed to enhance the vivid display. I sat down with my friends and Poppy walked around the table greeting each of them in turn, enjoying the attention they gave her. For some reason, she trotted straight past Samantha.

'It's just that she doesn't know you,' I said, hiding my surprise.

As a rule, Poppy grabbed every opportunity to befriend people. Very rarely she took against someone, in which case she could become quite aggressive, as had happened with Alfie. It was rare for her to treat a stranger with complete indifference.

'She can probably smell my cats,' Samantha said.

Barry put his pint down abruptly and turned to her with a startled expression. 'You never told me you had a cat,' he exclaimed.

Samamantha smiled. 'I'm sure I did.'

'No, you didn't. Seriously, Sam, I had no idea.'

'I'm sure I must have told you,' she repeated breezily. 'Actually I've got three,' she added. 'Two beautiful Persians and a tabby. You're going to love them. Everyone does.'

Barry nodded uneasily. Samantha continued to talk blithely about her pets, seemingly oblivious to Barry's discomfort. The conversation moved on and we passed a pleasant evening. As darkness fell, Richard and I walked back to the lane together with Poppy trotting ahead of us. Dana had already gone to bed by the time I arrived home. I turned in early as well, wondering whether she was really as tired as she was making out, or if she was avoiding me after our conversation about Alfie.

The following morning, Dana was not at home when I woke up. Hoping she had gone to a job interview, I wondered why she hadn't mentioned she was going out. Then I remembered how upset she had been the previous evening. Soon after she had calmed down, I had gone out. Even so, she could have left me a note and at first I was annoyed by her thoughtlessness. When she didn't answer her phone, I grew worried that she had been seriously upset by hearing about my encounter with Alfie. Suspecting I had been tactless to mention it, I resolved to try and discuss the situation with her when I had finished work.

I was serving a breakfast when Hannah hurried out of the kitchen, looking flustered, and hissed at me to go to the kitchen as soon as possible. Wondering what baking disaster could have prompted such unusual agitation, I made my way to the kitchen. Hannah rarely botched her baking, but it was not completely unheard of for scones or buns to burn. Usually she laughed off such blunders, which had happened quite a few times when I had first started working with her and she had let me help in the kitchen. These days, our roles were more distinct. She worked in the kitchen while I served at tables. We had found our own rhythm and it worked.

A shrouded figure was standing by the back door, poised as if ready to flee. Seeing me, Dana threw off her scarf and stared at me, her eyes like hollow pits. Trembling all over, she drew in a deep shuddering breath.

'Dana!' I cried out in surprise. 'What are you doing here?'

'Be quiet,' she replied in a fervent whisper. She took a step towards me and spoke almost under her breath, so that her words were difficult to distinguish. 'He got hold of me.'

'Alfie?' I asked her.

'Alfie.' She spat the name out as if it stung her lips.

'What happened?'

'I'll tell you about it,' she assured me, 'but not here, not now. As long as I'm here, the tea shop is in danger.'

'In danger? The tea shop? What do you mean?' Hannah spoke over our whispered conversation. 'Emily, what's going on?'

'Keep your voice down,' Dana hissed. 'There's no time to explain. Not now. Not here. I need to hide or he'll find me again, and next time I might not escape with my life.'

The bell jangled and Hannah hurried out to see who had come in.

'How can I help you?' I blurted out.

She shook her head. 'I don't think anyone can help me now. I shouldn't have come here but I wanted to see you again before I go. You've been so good to me, so kind.' She reached out and took my hand, interlocking her cold fingers with mine. 'You're the only true friend I have. Even my own mother is too afraid to speak to me. I couldn't go without saying goodbye. And now, I have to go. If he tracks me down, he'll kill me. He'll probably make it look like suicide.' She shuddered.

'He can't do that—' I began, but she interrupted me.

'I need to get as far away from here as possible, as quickly as I can, before he finds me.'

'But where will you go?'

She shook her head, helplessly.

'Let me help you,' I repeated. 'It will be safer than if you go out there on your own.'

Hannah returned and we were relieved to hear that the new arrival was one of our regular customers.

I turned to Dana and spoke quickly. 'Go to my next-door neighbour, Richard. Stay there for today, out of sight, and I'll come and find you this evening. Tell him I sent you. Don't worry, you'll be safe with him.'

'I'm not safe anywhere,' she replied sadly and turned and slipped out of the kitchen door.

Hannah wanted to know what Dana's visit meant, and why she had climbed over the gate and crossed the yard to enter through the back door. That was hardly the action of someone who was innocent, she said.

'If the police are looking for her again, then there must

be a reason. You shouldn't have sent her to Richard's. You might get him in trouble with the police. He's already had more than his fair share of dealing with them.'

She was alluding to a time when the police had suspected Richard of killing his wife, who had turned out to be living in London when her husband was arrested for murder.

'They might accuse him of being an accessory to whatever crime she's committed,' Hannah went on in a furious undertone. 'How do you know you can trust her? What are you playing at? It's one thing putting yourself in danger, but now you're involving other people.'

The bell jangled again and I scurried into the front room, pleased at the temporary respite. But I couldn't avoid Hannah for long and, in between serving customers, I filled her in about what Dana had told me. Hannah looked understandably worried.

'That sounds crazy,' she said. 'Do you believe what she told you?'

'I can see how far-fetched it all sounds, but we know a girl died at the fair, and Dana showed me the scar where Alfie threw boiling water at her.'

'If that's really what happened.'

I shrugged. 'Someone must have done it.'

'Are you sure Dana's telling you the truth? It's just that you can be so naïve.' She sighed. 'I like to give people the benefit of the doubt, but you must admit you can be a bit too trusting, and I worry about you.'

Admittedly, I had been gullible in the past, usually where boyfriends were concerned, but I was convinced Dana was telling me the truth. Although I hadn't known her for long, I had come to regard her as a friend, and I didn't believe she was lying to me. Besides, Poppy liked her, and she had proved herself a good judge of character. Promising to be careful, I turned my attention to the customers who had just arrived and the rest of the afternoon passed in a blur of activity. All the while, I was preoccupied with wondering what Dana was doing. The thought that she might put Richard in danger was alarming. On the other hand, if she hadn't gone to him, I might never find out what happened to her, or whether she was still alive.

When we finished work, I didn't stop for tea with Hannah but ran off to collect Poppy and hurry to Richard's house. Usually on our walk home Poppy was free to stop and sniff the ground whenever she wanted, but on this occasion I pulled her along the street as quickly as we could go, impatient to discover if Dana had followed my advice and gone to Richard's house. Poppy seemed to understand the urgency, and trotted quickly along without stopping. I wasn't sure whether to be relieved or concerned to discover Dana at Richard's house. We were soon sitting in his back garden with a large pot of tea and a selection of cakes and scones which I had brought with me, thanks to Hannah's generosity. With a sigh, Dana began. For Richard's benefit, she repeated what she had already told me about her early life growing up on the fairground, and how she had intended to marry Alfie until his violent behaviour had horrified her. She described how she had finally realised her life was in danger when he had thrown boiling water at her. She broke down in tears when she told us how her father had been killed after he had undertaken to protect her from Alfie.

'Alfie is a maniac,' she insisted. 'He won't tolerate anyone disagreeing with him. He can be a real charmer, but anyone who crosses him suffers for it. He attacked me and tried to kill me for standing in his way, he poisoned my father for thwarting him, and no doubt he murdered Paris when she tried to leave him.'

Richard looked thoughtful as he listened in silence. When Dana finished, he spoke solemnly, advising her to go straight to the police.

Dana shook her head with a sigh. 'The police? They won't protect me. They suspect me of killing Paris, even though they only questioned me in the first place because Alfie must have accused me of killing her. No doubt he said I hated her because he had abandoned me for her, and my jealousy had resulted in my attacking her in a fit of rage. But I can promise you I was no more guilty of assaulting her and throwing her off the big wheel than you are. I hadn't had any contact with Alfie for years. How could I still be harbouring a grudge against a girl who had been no more than a child when I left the fair? It doesn't make sense, does it? Anyway, the police couldn't find a shred of evidence to support Alfie's accusation so they let me go, but I think they're still suspicions of me. I'm not sure it would be a good idea for me to rely on the police to help. They made it perfectly clear what they thought about people like me. No, it's better if I just disappear.'

'I'm sure that's not true,' Richard said thoughtfully. 'Are you sure the prejudice is coming from the police?'

'You can't let him get away with it,' I burst out.

'What else can I do?' Dana asked, stroking Poppy's head sadly.

'I really think you should go to the police,' Richard insisted. 'If this man is guilty of murder, we have to do everything in our power to see he's arrested and brought to trial.'

'Richard's right,' I said. 'You can't just scarper and let Alfie get away with murder. Hide in the village while we plan what to do next. Whatever happens, we have to make sure he's punished for his crimes.'

'Hide in the village?' she repeated wonderingly. 'I can't do that. It's not safe for me here.'

'You must come back with me,' I said.

Richard gave me a worried glance but he didn't say anything, and I wondered if I was stupid to offer to shelter Dana again.

'No, I can't stay with you,' Dana replied. 'I've already brought you enough trouble. Or do you want another broken window? It could be something worse next time.'

At that point, Richard stood up with an air of decisiveness. 'You must stay here in my house,' he said to Dana. 'No one will think of looking for you here. No one even knows we've met. Now let's go inside. You'll be safe here.'

Dana frowned. 'Safe?' she repeated. 'I can never be safe while he's at large.'

'You'll be safe here,' Richard repeated. I wondered if he believed that, or if he was trying to protect me.

'What if someone saw her coming here?' I asked.

'No one followed me here,' she said slowly. 'I made sure of that. But I only came here to say goodbye properly to Emily. I should go now.'

Richard persuaded her to stay, at least for one night. He told her she would put herself at unnecessary risk if she tried to leave the village without careful preparation. It wasn't as if she had anywhere to go. In the end, she agreed to wait until the morning before leaving, disguised in his clothes. He promised to give her some money.

'And then I'm going to get as far away from here as I can,' she said. 'I'll go somewhere he'll never find me.'

'Where?' I asked her.

She shook her head. 'I don't know yet, but I'll think of something. I've escaped from him once before, and he's not going to get me now. I'm not going to be his next victim.'

13

IT MIGHT HAVE BEEN ingenuous of me, but I felt buoyed up by Richard's intervention in my new friend's problems. When he assured her she would be safe under his protection, I believed him. There was something reassuring about his quiet confidence. Dana was adamant no one had observed her going to Richard's house and, as long as Alfie had no idea she was there, we all agreed she and Richard would both be safe. She suggested it would be best if I didn't visit her in daylight, and I agreed to go there after dark, and even then only when I was sure no one was watching me.

'You'll have to be careful,' Dana said. 'I couldn't bear it if Richard was attacked because of me.'

'Don't worry,' I assured her. 'Poppy's bound to warn us if Alfie's lurking anywhere nearby.'

Poppy woke up and wagged her tail.

Richard and I agreed to avoid drawing attention to our friendship, but we thought it would be safe enough to see each other in the pub. Alfie might walk into the bar at any moment, but as long as we were with our friends, there was no reason for him to suspect Richard and I had formed a pact to keep Dana hidden away. That night I went to sleep feeling slightly less worried than I had been for a while. Dana was safe for now, but we still had to form a plan to make sure that continued. Somehow, we had to expose Alfie as a killer who had poisoned Dana's father and thrown Paris from the wheel to her death. As well as wanting Dana to be safe, I was determined that Alfie would not escape justice. As yet I had no idea how we were going to achieve our goal, but I knew we had to find a way to convince the police he was guilty of murder.

The next morning, my phone rang as Poppy and I were on our way to Jane's house. Poppy was trotting happily along, stopping to smell the weeds and grass, and snapping at the occasional bee that buzzed past on its busy journey from flower to flower. It was still quite early, and nascent heat hovered in the air. Soon, I would need to be careful that the pavements were not too hot for Poppy's little feet. Seeing that Hannah was calling me, I checked the time but I wasn't late for work. Expecting her to ask me to go to Maud's village shop on my way, I answered, but Hannah was crying so hard she could barely talk.

'What's wrong?' I asked her, with a suffocating sense of dread.

Seeing me stop, Poppy crouched at my feet and gazed up at me quizzically, her head on one side. Hannah mumbled incomprehensibly. Something was obviously very wrong.

'Has something happened to Adam?' I asked. 'Are you ill? What is it? Is it Richard?'

'The tea shop,' she mumbled. 'The tea shop.'

'I'm on my way,' I told her.

Abandoning my route to Jane's house, I hurried towards the tea shop, dragging Poppy with me. We arrived too early for Hannah to have opened the door and turned the sign around. If I was surprised to see the blinds were still drawn, that was nothing compared to the scene that greeted us when we entered. Tables had been overturned, chairs lay strewn around the room, and fragments of smashed plates and cups lay everywhere. Picking Poppy up so she couldn't hurt herself on any shards of broken crockery, I gazed around in stunned silence. Returning to my senses, I crunched my way cautiously across numerous splinters of china to the kitchen where I found Hannah leaning over the sink, shaking. Hearing me behind her, she turned and flung her arms around me, nearly crushing Poppy who let out a yelp in protest.

Hannah released me. 'Sorry, Poppy,' she cried out, laughing and crying at the same time. She paused to stroke Poppy's head, still sobbing.

Of the two of us, Hannah was always the calm one, frequently reassuring me that everything was going to be fine, however hopeless it might seem. Seeing her so distraught was a shock, forcing me to pull myself together in an instant. Briskly, I told her to get busy brewing a pot of tea. After a restorative hot drink, I said, we would set to work clearing up the mess. Between the two of us, I was confident it wouldn't take long to return the tea shop to its usual neat and welcoming state. Our aim was to open up in time to serve afternoon tea, in order to minimise the loss of custom.

'We'll keep at it until everything's back to normal,' I said.

Wiping her eyes and sniffing back her sobs, Hannah nodded. But before we did anything, I handed Poppy to Hannah and pulled out my phone to take photos of all the damage for an insurance claim, including the broken side window through which intruders had gained access to the tea shop. We agreed that the vandalism would have to be reported to the police and Hannah said she would call them, and an emergency glazier, while I was taking Poppy to Jane's house, out of harm's way. Relieved that she had recovered from her initial shock and was being practical, I left, promising to be back as soon as possible. It would be pointless to try and hide what had happened from Jane, but I assured Hannah I would play it down to avoid worrying her mother unnecessarily.

Hannah nodded. 'It's only a few plates,' she said, with a brave smile.

She appeared to have rallied. Nevertheless, I was keen not to leave her alone for long, and raced to Jane's house. Seeming to understand the need to hurry, Poppy scampered beside me without once stopping to sniff at weeds or water the grass. Jane was surprised to see us. 'I thought you weren't coming,' she said, a hint of reproof in her voice.

Apologising for being late, I gave her a sketchy account of what had happened. Seeing her about to panic, I reassured her that Hannah was fine and the damage was minimal. She immediately offered to help, but Poppy and Lily couldn't be allowed in the tea shop until the floor had been thoroughly swept and washed free of all splinters of broken china.

'But who was it?' she wanted to know. 'Who could have wanted to trash the tea shop? It doesn't make sense. What were they hoping to achieve with such senseless vandalism?'

I shook my head. 'I expect it was kids, chucking a stone to break the window.'

'What about the smashed plates?'

'I dare say they were chancing their luck, hoping to find some cash in the till.'

But I had a strong suspicion this was no random attack. Whoever had flung a rock through my window had not given up on their persecution of Dana's friends.

'It was probably those fairground workers,' Jane muttered, scowling. 'I hope the police catch them, whoever they are, and throw the book at them. You say they broke some of Hannah's plates?'

I nodded.

'What a pity,' she said. 'And what a mean stupid thing to do, smashing her lovely crockery like that.'

While we were talking, Jane's little puppy was jumping up at her and yelping shrilly, trying to attract her attention.

'It's mindless,' I agreed. 'That's why we think it was probably kids. No professional burglar would risk attracting attention, or waste time, by making such a racket for something so unprofitable. I mean, what could they possibly gain from smashing plates? Anyway, I'd best get back and help Hannah with the clearing up. We're hoping to open this afternoon and she might want to close late if we're busy, to make up for missing the morning. Depending on how it goes, and how long we stay open, I might be late picking Poppy up this evening, if that's all right.'

'Yes, of course. I hope they don't leave a mess dusting for fingerprints,' Jane replied, shaking her head. 'Poor Hannah. I wish I could be there to help. Do tell her I'd go with you if I could, but I have this little one to think of.' She lifted Lily up and nuzzled her face.

Poppy barked.

'And you,' Jane smiled, reaching down to stroke Poppy's head. 'And now, I'd better let them out in the garden,' she added, with a smile.

By the time I returned to the tea shop, Hannah had begun tidying up. The tables were the right way up, and the chairs had all been wiped and were neatly stacked along one wall, making it easier to wash the floor. As we collected the largest pieces of broken china, Hannah was relieved to discover the breakages were not as extensive as she had first suspected. Despite appearances, only about a dozen plates and one tea cup had been smashed. We worked in silence all morning. As we were sitting down for a rest and a cup of tea, Barry arrived with a female constable and a few colleagues. Two fingerprint officers set to work. Irritatingly, after leaving smears of sooty dust on the door and tables, they did not hold out much hope the culprits would be found.

'It's unusual for intruders not to wear gloves,' a young officer explained.

Hannah and I exchanged an exasperated glance, but neither of us asked why they were spending time dusting for nonexistent fingerprints, adding their dirty marks to the mess we had to clean up.

'Several such incidents have been reported recently,' the officer told us.

'I'm afraid there's been a spate of break-ins since the fair's been held here,' Barry said grimly. 'That's not to say the showmen are involved,' he added quickly. 'The fair attracts visitors from all over the surrounding area, and with so many people descending on the village, there are bound to be a few wrong 'uns. The last thing we want is fights breaking out between the fairground community and the locals.'

The female constable took down a statement from Hannah. I had nothing to add, other than to show them the photos on my phone which they studied without comment. At last they left and, after a quick bite of lunch, Hannah and I set to work again. At first we had been afraid the tea shop was wrecked, but the vandalism turned out to be fairly minor: just a few broken plates, the loss of a morning's turnover, and a horrible feeling of violation. The ovens still worked, and nothing of any significance had been damaged. We spent another hour sweeping and cleaning, restoring the tea shop to its customary orderly condition, and a glazier came to take measurements and board up the broken pane. At last we were finished in time for our usual teatime rush. We were exhausted, but satisfied with the result of our efforts. With a triumphant grin, Hannah turned the sign around and unlocked the door.

Hannah was in the kitchen when Adam arrived. He glared around wildly, demanding to know where she was. She emerged and ran to embrace him, assuring him that she was fine and, thanks to my efforts, the tea shop had opened in time for the teatime customers. Adam demanded to know how this could have happened and Hannah pointed to the boarded up window where intruders had broken the glass and reached in to open the door.

Usually mild-mannered and cheerful, Adam was incandescent. 'I've been telling you for years that you need to put a proper lock on the door,' he told her, trembling with anger. He was no stranger to trouble, having seen his father accused of murdering his mother. But this incident at the tea shop seemed to have made him snap.

Hannah's lip quivered.

'It's not her fault,' I couldn't help butting in. 'These vandals were criminals. They would have found a way in however well locked and bolted the door was.'

Adam shook his head. 'You may be right, but we are to blame for making it easy for them to get in.'

Hannah bowed her head. 'I know,' she said. 'That's why I haven't bothered to make a claim on the insurance. They'll wriggle out of paying and, to be honest, there isn't much to claim for, just a broken window and a few broken plates. By the time I pay the excess, and they hike up my premiums, it won't be worth it. But you're right, Adam. A locksmith has already been to see what he can do and he's ordered security locks which he should be able to fit tomorrow, to the front and back doors. And a burglar alarm company is coming to fit an alarm next week. It's going to be a hassle, and an additional expense, but I think we have to do it.' She sighed. 'It's a horrible world.'

I felt guilty, suspecting that I had brought this trouble on Hannah, but comforted myself by thinking that maybe it was just as well. While it had been inadequately protected by proper locks and an alarm system, the tea shop had always been vulnerable to burglars and other intruders. But it was hard to convince myself that my dangerous friendship with Dana had really benefited Hannah.

'I'm sorry,' I murmured as I left.

I tried not to think about Dana's warning that Rosecroft was unprotected without an alarm or a ring camera.

14

THAT EVENING, I WAS wary on my way home from Jane's house. I had seen how lithe Alfie was, darting easily along alleyways and over walls. If he wanted to stalk me, he could probably do so quite easily. Despite trusting that Poppy would bark if Alfie was near, I was nevertheless scared in case he was following me. It was a beautiful summer evening, and still light, but I couldn't enjoy the walk along the lane and let out a sigh of relief when we were home. As soon as it was dark we set off, walking past Richard's house several times to make sure no one was watching us. Poppy seemed perfectly happy, and didn't bark once. Even so, I made a show of going through the gate to Rosecroft before returning to the street. Picking Poppy up, I held her close to prevent her making a sound, and stole through Richard's gate. Having hurried up the path, I pressed myself against the front door, still clutching Poppy tightly in my arms to keep her quiet. There was no sign of anyone lurking in the shadows, and Poppy seemed calm. All the same, when Richard opened the door I held my breath and slipped inside without saying a word. Not until Richard had closed the door behind us did I breathe again.

Dana was waiting for us in the living room, looking apprehensive. Poppy ran to her and rolled over for a belly rub. For a moment, Dana relaxed, absorbed in Poppy's happiness.

'If only people were as easy to please as you are,' she murmured, leaning down and blowing a kiss at Poppy.

'People are much more complicated,' I said.

'More's the pity,' Richard agreed.

He fetched a tray with glasses and a bottle of wine and we listened to the faint glugging sound as he poured it.

'I thought this might help us to relax,' he explained, handing us each a glass. 'Life has become a little too stressful for you at the moment.'

It wasn't clear if he was talking to me or Dana, but his words could have been addressed to either of us.

'And this is for you,' he said, placing a saucer of water on the floor and pulling a dog treat from his pocket with a flourish, like a conjurer. 'You didn't think I'd forget you, did you? Now,' he went on, straightening up and going over to a chair, 'are you going to tell us exactly what's going on? There's a rumour flying around that there's been trouble at the tea shop. Tell me that's not true.'

Dana gasped when she heard what had happened. It was hard to believe she had heard nothing about it, such a long time seemed to have elapsed since Hannah had called to tell me the tea shop had been broken into. Richard explained his decision to say nothing to Dana until the rumour was confirmed. News was so often exaggerated in the village, and he was afraid Dana would rush out of the house to see Hannah, if he told her what he had heard. He had thought it wiser for her to remain out of sight, at least until we had discussed what she ought to do next.

While she had been working at the newspaper, she had enjoyed some protection from her enemy because she had a platform from where she could speak to the world. Now she had no such voice and was hiding in the shadows.

Dana was devastated to hear how the tea shop had been trashed. She refused to accept that the attack was not her fault.

'First Rosecroft, and now the tea shop,' she wailed, 'and it's all because of me. My presence is a blight on the lives of anyone who befriends me. You have to distance yourselves from me, for your own protection and for the sake of your friends.' She looked around wildly. 'Who will be next? I can't stay here, Richard, it's too dangerous for you to associate with me. Anyone could be watching. I have to leave right now.'

She leaped to her feet. Poppy barked in protest. Richard and I immediately urged her to sit down. Richard assured her she was safe at his house, while I wanted to know where she proposed to go right then, at the end of the day. With a sigh of resignation she sat down and resumed petting Poppy who settled back at her feet, her tail beating a gentle tattoo on the carpet. Richard refilled our glasses and we sat sipping our wine in silence for a few moments.

'This is excellent,' Dana said appreciatively. 'I don't deserve to be treated like this.'

'Yes, you do,' I told her. 'You're entitled to enjoy yourself as much as anyone. We all know you've done nothing wrong. Dana, you're the victim in this situation, more than anyone. Now, we need to work out what we're going to do. Somehow we have to find a way to expose Alfie for what he is. If only we could prove he was behind the attacks on Rosecroft and the tea shop.'

Dana shook her head. 'He's far too crafty to be caught out. He'll have made sure he's well protected. Even if we accused him, there'd be at least one person in the community willing to come forward and give him an alibi for the time of Paris's murder.'

'You can't know that,' I protested. 'A woman died. Won't everyone want to see her killer brought to justice?'

'You don't understand. Even if they don't all close ranks against an official investigation, it only takes one or two of them to corroborate his lies and he'll be in the clear. Not all travelling showpeople trust the police.'

'Yourself included,' I murmured, remembering how fiercely Dana had resisted reporting my broken window to the police.

Dana lowered her head and didn't reply, and I felt momentarily abashed for having reminded her of what had happened.

Perhaps it was my regret at having mentioned our disagreement, or it might have been Richard's wine that was making me bold, but I was suddenly sure the time had come to act.

'We have to set a trap for Alfie,' I said firmly. 'We can't just sit around waiting for his next attack. We have to seize the initiative.'

Richard looked puzzled, but Dana shook her head. 'There's nothing we can do,' she said. 'He's too powerful.'

'No, he isn't,' I replied. 'He may be powerful within his own community, but that's the extent of his influence. Once we expose him, he'll have nowhere to hide.' I smiled at Dana, who sat frowning and shaking her head. 'We need to catch him out and force him to confess his crimes. And we need to record him secretly.' I leaned forward in my chair. 'But before we make our plans, are you absolutely sure he killed Paris?'

Dana scowled. 'If you doubt me, why are you helping me, when you know my presence here is a threat to you and all your friends? No one has the guts to come out and say it, but everyone knows he's guilty.'

'Yes, it certainly seems that way.' Still, I had only Dana's word for it that Alfie was responsible for killing Paris and vandalising my house and Hannah's tea shop. 'Is that all the proof I'm going to get that he's responsible for what's happened? That everyone agrees he's guilty although no one can prove it, and most of his associates won't admit the truth. If I'm going to stick my neck out, and possibly risk danger to see Alfie arrested, I need to be absolutely sure he's guilty.'

She nodded. 'Do you believe me when I say he assaulted me, several times, before I left him, and Paris was living with him when she died?'

I nodded, and Richard murmured that he trusted Dana. Having spent a day together, it appeared that Richard and Dana had struck up a friendship. Like me, he seemed satisfied she was no criminal.

'My conviction that he killed her is based on my own experience, but no, I can't prove it.' Dana stared at me with a worried expression. 'I suppose there's always a chance I could be wrong.'

'If we're going to get proof, we're going to need help from someone at the fair,' I said, with a vague plan forming in my head. 'Is there anyone there you can count on not to betray you to Alfie?'

'There's only one person at the fair that I trust, and that's my mother, Sarah. I would trust her with my life, but we can't be seen together so we would have to meet in secret. There's no way I'm going to put her at risk. If I can talk to her without any possibility of anyone there finding out, she might be able to confirm my suspicion. I can't promise she'd be willing to talk to me, but I think she would. We've only seen each other a few times since I quit the fair, but she's still my mother. I left with her blessing. She knows what Alfie did to me.'

She made an involuntary movement, resting her right hand against the scar on her left arm where she had been scalded. I saw no reason to question what she was saying, and it could do no harm for her to try and speak to her mother. Dana and Richard began discussing how a secret meeting could be arranged, and I offered to try and convey a message to Sarah without anyone seeing. As long as the message was sent anonymously, with no mention of where Dana was hiding out, we didn't think it could do any harm. Dana told me in exact detail where Sarah lived by herself in a faded blue trailer parked at the edge of the fairground encampment. Somehow I had to contact her without anyone else knowing about it. Richard was keen to help in any way he could, but Dana and I both agreed he should stay away from the fair as long as Dana was hiding in his house. It would not do for him to attract any unwanted attention.

Assuring Dana that I would find a way to send her mother to a secret meeting place yet to be agreed, I slipped out of the house, once again holding Poppy in my arms. I held her jaws closed so she could not bark, even if a fox ran across our path. We made our way safely back home, where I locked the door with a shiver of relief. Even the short walk from my next-door neighbour's house to Rosecroft felt risky. That night, I lay awake for a long time puzzling over how to send a message to Sarah. Only when Poppy jumped up on my bed and nuzzled my feet, did an idea finally occur to me. I leaned forward and rubbed her belly.

'Well done,' I said. 'Good girl, Poppy. Good girl. We'll do this together.'

Poppy settled down at the foot of the bed and closed her eyes, growling softly. Sometimes she sounded like a cat, purring with contentment.

The fair had not been in operation for over two weeks, and some villagers were sharing the story that the showpeople were preparing to leave and would soon be gone. The same rumour had been circulating ever since the fairground workers had been forbidden to leave Ashton Mead. It had become one of the recurring topics of conversation among customers at the tea shop.

'They can't be gone soon enough,' I heard one elderly customer say.

'Be patient,' her companion counselled. 'They won't be here for much longer.'

'Is it true they're being paid to stay here?' someone else asked.

'They've been clamouring for what they call recompense,' another customer added indignantly. 'Recompense, I ask you. These days everyone expects something for nothing.'

Her friend said she had heard the same thing.

'Well, they are losing their livelihood while they're stuck here,' the elderly woman's companion pointed out. 'I dare say they're as keen to leave as we are to see them go. It's worse for them, when you think about it, because all the time they're stuck here they're unable to set up the fair anywhere else.'

'I blame the police,' another woman said. 'They're the ones keeping them here.'

15

PREOCCUPIED WITH MY MISSION, I struggled to focus at work the next day. Hannah would have tried to dissuade me from going ahead if she had learned of my plan, and she wouldn't have met with much resistance. Going to the fairground alone would have been risky even if I hadn't been friendly with an opponent of a suspected killer. Although I did my best to hide my nerves, Hannah realised something was on my mind and challenged me about it. I felt guilty for insisting everything was fine, when that was far from true, but she accepted my assurance.

'I'm just tired,' I said. 'It's been a busy few days.'

'It certainly has,' she agreed with a grudging smile. 'Let's hope the fairground workers move away soon so life can get back to normal. There's been far too much drama recently for my liking. And everyone's fed up with the police prowling around morning, noon and night.'

She was exaggerating, although it was true that since the murder Barry had no longer been the sole police presence in the village. The locals had learned to recognise plain clothes detectives visiting Ashton Mead.

'I don't know what they're hoping to find out by questioning us again,' Hannah went on, repeating a grumble that many of our customers had voiced. 'It's the outsiders they ought to be focusing on, not us. The fair's where the murder took place, and the killer was obviously one of them. They just happened to be here in Ashton Mead when it happened.'

At last the working day drew to a close and I went to fetch Poppy from Jane's house. My scheme was beginning to weigh heavily on me, and my nerves were frayed. When Jane asked me about my plans for the evening, I gave a guilty start. Fortunately she was watching Lily, and didn't notice my reaction. We were in the garden, enjoying the relative cool after the heat of the day. Lily was dragging around a stuffed fluffy fox that was nearly as big as she was. Poppy darted forward to snatch it from her, and Lily gave chase. Poppy was faster than Lily, but Poppy paused to make the fox squeak, and Lily ran forward to retrieve it. Jane laughed at them and I lingered, watching the dogs interact. I realised I was procrastinating, apprehensive about what lay ahead.

Jane offered to make a pot of tea. 'It's such a lovely evening,' she said. 'You don't have to rush off, do you?'

On another occasion I might have accepted, but I shook my head and stood up. Jane's invitation had galvanised me and I suddenly resolved to reach the fair as soon as possible. Partly I was keen to get there before I got cold feet, but I was also anxious to complete my task before nightfall. As long as it was still light, if anyone challenged me I could claim to be taking Poppy for a walk. Before the arrival of the fair, we often used to wander around on the grassy slopes near the river. It was a public area, even though the showpeople had been forced to make their camp there. Muttering an excuse, I said goodbye to Jane and set off with Poppy trotting beside me.

As we drew near to the river, muted sounds could be heard coming from the trailers and caravans: voices calling out, tinny music, people arguing, and the sound of laughter. Somewhere a dog barked, a deep throated threatening sound. Poppy bristled. Picking her up, I hushed her and made my way past the row of vehicles to a rundown blue trailer parked at the far end of the fairground encampment. If this was the wrong vehicle, I would have to abort my secret attempt to contact Dana's mother without anyone else spotting me. So far, I was plausibly just going for a walk, but that was about to change and I might soon land myself in serious trouble.

After glancing fearfully all around, I darted up the steps to the door of the trailer and knocked softly. Putting Poppy down, I let go of her lead and instructed her to stay. Assuming I was in the right place, the success of my plan depended on her obedience. Leaping down the steps, I slipped into the shadows between two trailers and crouched down to watch and wait, praying the dog we had heard earlier would not come along and find me there. For my idea to work, Dana's mother had to be alone in her vehicle, and she had to discover Poppy on her doorstep. Should anyone else come across Poppy first, things might go horribly wrong, and not just for me. Focused on delivering a message to Sarah, I hadn't considered all the possible consequences of my actions. Only now did it occur to me that I had overlooked the risk to Poppy. I was about to abandon my ill-conceived scheme when the door of the trailer flew open. I started forward and cried out, but my volte-face came too late. By the time I reached the steps, Poppy had already dashed inside and the door had closed. I held my breath, hoping Sarah would let Poppy out again straightaway. I had practised what to say, over and over again: 'Have you seen a small dog? She's a Jack Tzu called Poppy.'

Jack Tzus were a sought-after breed, but she was wearing a collar, a clear indication that she had an owner and was microchipped. It ought to be virtually impossible to steal her because she was traceable, but now that she had vanished inside a trailer, any rational analysis of the situation gave me little comfort. All I could think of was that a stranger had taken Poppy into her home, and I might never see her again – and I had deliberately set this up. Even now, Sarah was probably making a fuss of Poppy who might believe I had deliberately given her away. Worse than that, I didn't know if Sarah had been alone in her trailer when Poppy had run in. The thought that Alfie might be in there made me shudder with fear. I didn't even know for sure that I had brought Poppy to the right trailer.

While I was prevaricating, I heard footsteps and cheery whistling, and a voice greeted me.

'Hello, who do we have here, skulking in the shadows? Looking for me, are you, gorgeous?'

I spun round to face Alfie. My initial feeling was one of relief that he wasn't in Sarah's trailer, but that was quickly superseded by fear. Restraining myself from retorting that he was the last person I wanted to see, I braced myself for whatever came next.

'I knew you'd come looking for me,' Alfie went on, leering at me. 'Give me a minute. I just need to send my girl packing and we'll have the caravan to ourselves.'

'No, no,' I stammered, backing away from him. 'I'm looking for my dog.' Almost without thinking, I slipped into my rehearsed speech. 'We were going for a walk and she ran off and now she's disappeared. She must be in one of these trailers. I thought I'd start at one end of the group and work my way along. It's possible she's gone home,' I added. 'If she has, then she'll wait for me there. But I don't want to leave without checking here first.'

Alfie was watching me speculatively as I talked and I hoped he didn't realise how scared I was.

'Once I've found my dog, then maybe we can go to your caravan,' I added wildly, making a desperate attempt to look as though I was flirting. My smile must have looked fake, but I persevered. 'As long as my dog's missing, I can't think about anything else.'

Out of the corner of my eye, I saw the door of Sarah's trailer swing open and heard Poppy bark. She came running down the steps towards me. As I grabbed her lead, I saw that the small bag I had attached to her collar earlier had gone. Oblivious to my relief, Alfie reached down to pet Poppy who drew back, snarling at him.

'Whoa,' he cried out, laughing, but looking disconcerted. 'Maybe you can come back later, without your dog.'

'Not tonight,' I replied firmly.

Just then, a woman came out of the trailer, waving her hands at Alfie as though he was a gnat buzzing around her head. She was wearing jeans and a baggy sweatshirt. A red scarf was wound round her head, and large hooped gold earrings swung from her ears. She had Dana's piercing dark eyes and prominent nose, but she was shorter than her daughter and her shoulders were more bowed. To my surprise, a huge Alsatian lumbered down the steps behind her. It hadn't occurred to me that Sarah might have a dog of her own in her trailer, and I shuddered at yet another potential danger I had sent Poppy in to face. Ignoring one another, the two dogs both began growling and barking at Alfie, their raucous chorus carried on the evening air.

In the distance, a man's voice yelled at us to 'Keep those bloody dogs quiet!' but neither Sarah nor I made any attempt to stop the barking. Staring at the Alsatian, Alfie stumbled backwards in obvious alarm. The animal wasn't on a leash, and could have pounced at any moment. I scooped Poppy up in my arms, hoping Sarah was able to control her dog.

'You keep that vicious brute away from me or I'll have it put down!' Alfie shouted at Sarah, his eyes glued to the Alsatian. 'That animal is a bloody menace.'

Poppy's barking grew more frenzied, and she wriggled frantically, as though she was determined to appear as threatening as the Alsatian. However ferociously she barked, Poppy was tiny beside Sarah's dog, whose snarling jaws were truly terrifying. While Poppy might perhaps have given Alfie a nasty bite on the leg if she hadn't been on her lead, the larger dog was unrestrained and could have ripped him to shreds effortlessly.

'Oh, get away with you, Alfie, and stop pestering that young girl,' Sarah replied, sounding irritated. 'Any more of your nonsense and I'll set Juno on you and serve you right.' She laughed as he cowered. 'Get away with you now, or I'll be having words with your grandmother. Now get yourself home to your supper and give us all some peace.'

With that, she turned her back on me and Alfie, and stomped back up into her trailer, her massive bitch at her heels. She hadn't looked at me once or acknowledged my presence in any way. Alfie cast a final look at me and

Poppy and slipped away between the vehicles to vanish in the gathering dusk. We ran all the way home and, as soon as the front door shut behind us, I sank down on the floor, shaking. Poppy came over and nuzzled me, whimpering softly until I petted her.

'Well done, Poppy,' I whispered. 'Well done, clever girl.'

She wagged her tail as if to reassure me that I had never been in any danger, with her there to defend me. But if Sarah's Alsatian had turned on us, there would have been little either of us could have done to save ourselves. I had failed in my job to protect Poppy.

'I'll never put you in danger again,' I promised her.

She gazed at me quizzically, and let out a single bark.

'I mean it. From now on, I'm going to take better care of you.'

Her response was to curl up on the floor and close her eyes. It was hard not to interpret that as her telling me she was not going to listen to any more of my nonsense.

Now I just had to hope Sarah had read the message concealed in the bag attached to Poppy's collar, and that she would meet Dana at the secret rendezvous that night.

16

At ten minutes to midnight, I set off. Poppy was eager to accompany me on my night time expedition, but it was too risky to take her with me. Foxes often roamed at night, and it was unrealistic to expect her to keep quiet. I had considered taking her with me so I could claim to be taking her for a walk if anyone spotted us, but on balance decided it was better to travel silently under cover of darkness. Wearing a navy coat, with a black scarf wound around my red hair, I crept down my front path and stole down the lane, walking at the side of the pavement to avoid being picked up in the glare of streetlights which had never before seemed so bright. As I reached the High Street, a bank of clouds drifted across the moon, shielding me to some extent, but I still kept to the edge of the pavement, pressing myself against the buildings whenever possible, and slipping along alleyways to avoid the lights.

Reaching the edge of the woods, I looked around but saw no movement. I called out very quietly. No one answered. I waited, but only the rustling of leaves overhead disturbed the silence. As I was wondering whether to wait or turn back and hurry home, a movement between the tree trunks caught my eye.

'Dana,' I whispered, 'is that you?'

'Emily?'

I joined her among the trees and we reassured each other that, as far as we could tell, no one had followed us to the meeting place.

'I hope my mother can find it,' she murmured.

The instructions on the message were clear, but Sarah wasn't local and it would be easy for her to miss the path to the woods in the darkness. It had seemed too hazardous for her to come to Rosecroft, or to Richard's house, but now I wondered whether the choice to meet in the woods had been sensible. It would be all too easy to miss one another in the darkness, even if she managed to find her way to the meeting point. And if anyone followed her, there was no knowing what might happen to us out here in the woods.

'Perhaps we should have met her at the pub,' I whispered, 'or at my house.'

But it was too late to go back and alter the decision now. All we could do was wait and hope Sarah would find us. The minutes ticked by and there was no sign of her. After half an hour, Dana was ready to give up and leave, but I urged her to wait a little longer. Sarah might have been delayed by someone spotting her as she was leaving her trailer, or she could have lost her way. We agreed to wait until one o'clock, before abandoning our post.

'This is all my fault,' I muttered. 'I should have chosen a more sensible place to meet. How could I have been such an idiot?'

Dana disagreed with me in a furious whisper, saying I had nothing to apologise for. She pointed out that we wouldn't have been trying to meet with her mother at all, were it not for my plan. She insisted that it had been ingenious of me to send Sarah a message attached to Poppy's collar, but I wasn't convinced. We had no way of knowing whether Sarah had read the message. Even if she had, she might judge it too risky to come to the rendezvous. And it was even possible that Alfie himself might turn up instead, if he had managed to intercept my instructions.

'My mother would never betray us,' Dana hissed.

But Alfie might have seen the message, without Sarah knowing he had found it. He could already be on his way to find us, and Poppy wasn't there to warn us of his approach. The prospect of being isolated in the woods with him made me shudder and I gazed at Dana's shadowy outline, and hoped I hadn't put us both in mortal danger.

It was ten to one when we heard the soft scraping of footsteps. I held my breath. Someone was panting nearby.

'Dana?' a voice murmured, so softly it could have been the breeze stirring the leaves in the branches above us. 'Dana?' This time there was no mistaking the sound of my friend's name being called in a low whisper. 'Are you there? For goodness' sake, answer me if you're there. We've been searching for you for ages and I've no idea if we're in the right place.'

'Mum?' Dana called out quietly.

In the darkness, I could just about make out Sarah's silhouette. Relief flooded through me. Not only were there now three of us, but Sarah had brought her Alsatian with her. Ambling along, Juno sniffed at the ground, panting audibly. I smiled with relief. Dana and I were no longer in any immediate danger from Alfie.

Dana and her mother ran into each other's arms and hugged, before Dana introduced me.

'You're the little dog's girl,' Sarah said. Her voice sounded kind. 'Where is she? Your little dog?'

I explained why I had left Poppy at home and Sarah nodded at me, her movement barely discernible in the darkness. Dana explained that I wanted to help her see Alfie convicted for the recent murder.

'Poor Paris,' Sarah replied. 'That swine deserves to be strung up for what he did to her. There's some of us would do it tomorrow, but he's got too many supporters, and no one wants to see the community split. It would be the end of us. So we just put up with it.'

'No,' I blurted out. 'You mustn't let him get away with it.'

'What else can we do? He's got too much influence. He's convinced the majority of people who work on the fair that it would be disastrous for us all if he was investigated. "I know there are those who want to see me locked up," he says. "But I'm innocent." Innocent my arse!' She snorted.

'Why does anyone listen to him?' I asked.

'A lot of them are taken in by his talk about his contacts on the councils who give us permission to pitch up,' Sarah replied. 'He has the knack of bamboozling people with his clever words.'

'He may be persuasive, but surely he's not the only one who can run the show,' I protested.

'True enough,' she replied. 'But Alfie's right about one thing. It would be disastrous if the police were to be involved. It doesn't take much imagination to picture the outcry there would be in the media about our itinerant community sheltering a coldblooded murderer. And the longer it goes on, the worse it will be for all of us if he's arrested. The public will think we all knew what he'd done and were deliberately sheltering him, and there'll be no one to prove otherwise. We'll be painted as lawless and wicked, and God only knows what else, as well as itinerant. It will be a witch hunt all over again. No one will want us and our fair anywhere near their towns and villages. Our livelihood is hanging on by a thread as it is. If Alfie's arrested and all this comes out in the open, there's a strong chance we won't survive the fallout. That's what keeps people silent. It's not loyalty to Alfie, it's fear for our future.'

I listened to her, shocked. 'No,' I repeated, when she paused to draw breath. 'You can't just sit back and let him get away with it.'

'There are those who think we don't have a choice, not if we want our way of life to continue.'

'You can't let him get away with murder,' I repeated firmly. 'What's going to stop him doing it again, if he thinks there are no repercussions?'

In the darkness, we heard Sarah heave a sigh. 'You're right, of course, and none of us would disagree with you, in principle, but it's just not that simple. It sounds dreadful, I know, but you can't begin to imagine the persecution it would threaten to unleash on us.'

'You're wrong about that,' I replied. 'This isn't the Middle Ages. There's a system of justice in place to protect the innocent as well as to punish the guilty.'

'It must be nice to be able to believe that,' Sarah said. 'But my community lives outside the protection of the law.'

'How can you expect to receive the protection of the law when you are deliberately sheltering a murderer?' I demanded angrily. 'You don't deserve society's protection.'

Juno growled softly.

Sarah turned to Dana. 'Is this what you brought me here for? To listen to your friend spout her naïve opinions? You, of all people, should know better. You know what life is like for us, how precarious our existence is.'

'Mother,' Dana said softly. 'I know what you're saying is true, but Emily's right. Alfie can't be allowed to get away with murder. He must be stopped, whatever the cost.'

'And how do you propose to do that?' Sarah asked. 'You know I can't help you even if I want to. I shouldn't even have come here. I only came to see you.' She reached out and touched Dana's cheek.

'Wait,' I said, reaching out to take her hand. Her dog growled another warning and I dropped my arm. 'How can we be sure that Alfie killed Paris?'

Sarah's eyes gazed at me, dark and bright in the moonlight. 'Oh, he killed her all right,' she burst out in a furious whisper. 'Everyone knows it, only they're too scared to admit it. He killed my Tommy, and he would have killed Dana too, if she hadn't got away. And now his new girlfriend Lizzie's starting to get cold feet. She told me she's worried she's making a mistake. It won't be long before he finds out she's thinking of leaving him and then God help her.' She hesitated before adding that she would help us if she could. 'But I daren't. How can I be responsible for ruining the lives of everyone I know, all my friends, all my family, everyone? But if you want to nail the bastard, I'll be cheering you on, whatever carnage follows.'

'There's only one thing we need you to do,' I told her. 'You have to help us. We can't do this without you.'

I listened while Dana and her mother had a whispered exchange. At last, they embraced tearfully and Sarah vanished into the darkness of the night, her huge dog loping at her side. When we were sure she would be back at the fairground camp, Dana and I walked back through the village together. We had completed our mission to meet her mother in secret, but Dana still needed to return to Richard's house unobserved. To our relief, no one else was abroad at two o'clock in the morning, and we reached the village without passing anyone. We stole cautiously along the lane, checking that we weren't being followed, before Dana slipped back into Richard's house and I went home to Poppy who greeted me with her customary enthusiasm while I removed my muddy shoes and hung up my coat.

Convinced that Alfie had killed Paris, it was time to put our plan into action. All it needed now was for me to see Alfie alone in his caravan when everything was in place, and coax a confession out of him.

'It's going to happen,' I told Poppy. 'We're going to see that vicious brute locked up. Lizzie and every other young woman working at the fair will be safe, and Dana will be able to see her mother whenever she wants to. I'm determined to make it happen.'

Poppy whimpered and wagged her tail halfheartedly, gazing up at me with a mournful expression.

'There's no need to look so worried,' I said. 'Everything's going to be fine, you'll see.'

Remembering how Sarah had described me as naïve, echoing Hannah's opinion of me, I hoped my confidence wasn't misplaced. Meanwhile, it was nearly three in the morning and I needed to get some sleep.

'Come on, Poppy, time for bed,' I said.

She stared at me in surprise. Clearly, she thought it was time to begin our day. Ignoring her fussing, I went upstairs and flung myself down on the bed. In the morning, I was surprised to discover that I had gone to sleep fully dressed. Poppy, who had been eager to go outside at three o'clock in the morning, was stretched out at my feet, fast asleep. She opened one lazy eye when I moved. A second later, she sprang off the bed, barking to go outside.

'Give me a minute, Poppy,' I laughed. 'You can't pretend you're desperate to go out, when you were fast asleep just a moment ago.'

17

THAT MORNING, HANNAH WAS surprised to see Poppy had come with me to the tea shop.

I couldn't explain that, while she might be too small to protect me from a killer, Poppy could at least warn me of his presence. Making a feeble and transparently fake excuse about wanting to spend more time with Poppy, I set to work laying the tables and wiping the mats. But Hannah's curiosity was not easily curbed. Throughout the day I was conscious of her watching me out of the corner of her eye. It was difficult to pretend everything was fine when every time the bell jingled, my breath caught in my throat in case Alfie had come looking for me. Hannah's conspicuous surveillance didn't help. All day I was almost unbearably tense and distracted, and I delivered the wrong orders to several tables.

'I asked for fruit scones,' one irate customer said. 'These scones don't have any raisins at all.' He pointed to a plain scone that he had sliced through. 'There's not a raisin to be seen.'

At the same time, another customer complained that she had been brought scones she hadn't ordered. 'Look at it,' she grumbled. 'It's full of raisins. I can't eat raisins. I never eat raisins.' She shuddered. 'There's no way I would have ordered these. Take them away and bring me the plain scones I asked for.'

Flustered, I could only apologise to the customers and hurry to rectify my errors.

'Emily, what's wrong with you today?' Hannah asked me, thoughtfully biting into one of the scones rejected by a customer. 'If I didn't know better, I'd suspect you were trying to sabotage my business.'

Laughing awkwardly, I turned away to hide my distress. Life was challenging enough without the risk of losing the goodwill of my best friend, not to mention my job. But despite our close friendship, I dared not tell Hannah about the plan I had devised with Dana and Sarah.

'It's all right,' Hannah reassured me, seeing my expression. 'We all have our off days. But it would be really great if you could pull yourself together and start taking orders down correctly, like you're being paid to do. Right now, I'd be better off running the place on my own than having you here to help.'

Fortunately we were kept busy most of the day, so she had no opportunity to quiz me about what was wrong. Since there was no need for me to rush off at the end of the day to collect Poppy, Hannah suggested we share a pot of tea as we often did after closing for the day. Having turned the sign around, she went to the kitchen to stack the dishwasher, leaving me to clear the last of the tables. We tidied up while the tea was brewing, and when we had finished, she invited me to sit down. I hesitated, but it would have seemed odd to refuse, so we sat together with a pot of tea and a plate of scones between us.

'I've been looking forward to this,' she said, as she poured the tea while I buttered a scone and avoided meeting her eye. 'Now, tell me exactly what's going on between you and my mother.'

'Me and Jane?' I repeated in astonishment. 'I've no idea what you're talking about. Why would anything be going on between us?'

'You refused to take Poppy to her house today and I want to know why. My mother's as much in the dark about it as I am. She phoned me this morning to ask me what was wrong. I assured her there must be a perfectly sensible explanation, but we both want to hear it. Is it anything to do with Lily?'

Flabbergasted, I shook my head. Seeing my astonishment, she changed her tack. 'What is it then, if it's not Lily?' she demanded. 'Is there something wrong with Poppy?' Aghast at the idea which had just occurred to her, she turned to look through the kitchen door at Poppy, who was sleeping peacefully in her basket in the corner by the door. Her ears twitched when she heard her name, but she didn't stir.

'Poppy's fine,' I assured Hannah.

'Well, what is it, then?'

'Nothing.' I took a bite of my scone. It was as light and tasty as Hannah's baking always was, yet I found it difficult to swallow.

'Something's going on and I want to know why you're holding out on me. Is it a man?' she added with a worried frown. 'Emily, tell me what's happened. Are you in trouble? Whatever it is, it can't be that bad. Talk to me. It never helps to bottle things up. Has my mother done something to upset you?'

I shook my head vehemently.

'Are you pregnant?'

I shook my head again. 'You couldn't be more wrong,' I replied, truthfully, almost laughing at the suggestion.

'Well, what is it then? Only there's clearly something going on. Why can't you tell me? We're friends, aren't we?' She was nearly in tears. 'Is it me? Have I done something to upset you? Emily, tell me what it is.'

'There is something on my mind,' I admitted, 'but it's nothing to do with you.' I hesitated, hating to see her so upset on my account.

She looked at me anxiously. 'Are you ill?' she whispered.

'No, no, I'm absolutely fine. Listen, if I tell you what's bothering me, will you promise to keep it to yourself? Seriously, Hannah, you can't tell anyone. Not even Adam.'

She nodded, wide-eyed with curiosity. She leaned forward, listening intently to my account of my suspicions of Alfie, and everything Dana had told me about him. I explained how important it was that something be done to stop him before he could kill again.

'And you thought you'd take it on yourself to meddle in matters that should be left to the police?' she said, with a resigned sigh. 'Oh, Emily, that's so typical of you. But what can we do if the people he travels with are determined to shield him? You said it yourself, they're prepared to lie to protect their reputation, even at the cost of letting a possible murderer go free.'

'I completely get why they're so paranoid,' I said. 'After centuries of persecution, it's understandable they don't trust the police. They're not exactly popular with the general public, and they're afraid opinion will turn against them even more if Alfie is exposed as a psychopath they've been shielding. But that doesn't mean no one should do anything to stop him.'

'This is all pure speculation,' she said. 'Do you really think you know more about this character, Alfie, than people who've known him all his life? And even supposing you're right which you have to admit is a longshot, at best, there's nothing we can we do about it. Seriously, Emily, this is nothing to do with us, and it could be dangerous if you try to interfere. You've already had your window smashed.' She didn't add that the tea shop had also been vandalised, although she might as well have done. 'I mean it, Emily. You can tell Barry about your suspicions but, apart from that, there's nothing we can do.'

'Not we,' I replied. 'Me. You mustn't tell anyone what I'm about to say.'

'Go on,' she urged me, without agreeing to keep my secret to herself.

'Promise me you won't tell anyone else.'

'First tell me what you're proposing to do. If you're thinking of putting yourself at risk from some violent maniac, then I'll go straight to the police, which is what you should be doing if you're serious about all this.'

'I'll be perfectly safe,' I lied. 'Sarah's helping me, and Alfie's terrified of her Alsatian. I can't say I blame him,' I added with a smile. 'Juno's huge. She's the kind of dog you want on your side.'

From the kitchen, we heard a fierce growl. 'And you're a force to be reckoned with too,' I called out to Poppy and laughed. 'She was growling in her sleep.'

'Go on,' Hannah urged me.

'Promise me,' I insisted.

'Yes, all right, as long as you're not proposing to do anything dangerous, I promise I won't tell anyone.'

Briefly I outlined my plan to her. It would be easy enough for me to arrange to see Alfie alone. He had already made a move on me. All I had to do was respond to his advances, and he was bound to invite me to his caravan so we could be alone together. Once there, I would wheedle the truth out of him while, unknown to him, I would be recording everything he said. Once I had his confession stored on my phone, I would go straight to the police.

'So you see, it's simple,' I concluded triumphantly.

'No, it's not simple,' Hannah burst out. 'It's an idiotic idea! Honestly, Emily, that's one of the stupidest things I've ever heard. Listen to me, if this man really is dangerous, you could be risking your life if you let him anywhere near you. Your only option is to walk away and have nothing whatsoever to do with him.'

She gasped when I told her I was determined to do the exact opposite of what she was suggesting. She rose to her feet, her face red with anger. Poppy jumped out of her basket and ran over to investigate what was going on. She looked from me to Hannah and back again, whimpering softly.

'Emily, how can you be so dumb?' Hannah continued. 'Do you really think he's going to blab about his crimes, for no reason? Why on earth would he do that? This isn't a Geraldine Steel murder mystery, this is real. A violent psychopath is more likely to assault you than confess his guilty secrets to you. And if he finds out what you're up to, he's going to do whatever he can to ensure you never share your suspicions with anyone else ever again. If it's true that he's already committed several murders, then you're going to end up as another of his victims if you carry on with this lunacy.'

To say I was disappointed in my friend was an under-statement. 'I'm doing it, and you can't stop me,' I said defiantly, hiding my apprehension.

Hannah was scowling, but at least she appeared to be listening to me.

'He can't be allowed to walk away scot-free,' I went on doggedly. 'Sarah's already convinced he's going to kill again.' I told her what Dana's mother had said about Alfie's current girlfriend, Lizzie. 'There are people in his community who would speak out if they weren't so afraid of him. Once Alfie's arrested, he won't be able to intimidate witnesses and they'll come forward and testify against him. With Alfie behind bars, I'm sure we'll be able to convince them that the media will treat them as heroes, not criminals, if they help get a murderer locked up. We have to get them on board, and we can only do that if we convince the police to take him seriously as a suspect. Clearly no one else is going to do it, so it has to be me.'

Having explained myself, I waited anxiously to hear what Hannah would say. At the same time, I was relieved at having shared my secret plan with her, and almost hoping she would dissuade me from going ahead.

Eventually Hannah sighed. 'Maybe you're right,' she conceded, and I forced myself to be pleased. 'If you're positive Alfie's guilty of murder, then I suppose it's fair enough that you feel compelled to do something about it. But what can you possibly do? I mean seriously? It's insane to think you can persuade him to confess. Be sensible, Emily. It's too dangerous. I refuse to sit by and let you throw yourself into his clutches like that.'

'You can't stop me.'

'Maybe not,' she conceded, 'but I can help you.'

It was my turn to be surprised. 'What?'

'Emily, you must realise you can't carry out this harebrained scheme by yourself. You're going to need all the help you can get. What if something goes wrong? He might spot that you're recording what he says. And even if it goes according to plan, which seems almost impossible, how do you intend to get away from him after he's confessed?'

I admitted that my exit strategy was one of the weak points in my scheme. We discussed my plan for some time, with Hannah insisting Alfie was unlikely to confess, and me insisting that he might. Eventually Hannah persuaded me that it would be foolhardy to meet Alfie, and hope to stay safe, all by myself. Accepting that I would need back up, I agreed to go to her house that evening, where she offered to host a meeting of our friends, Adam, Toby, Michelle and, probably most importantly, Barry. Between us we might come up with a scheme where we could outwit Alfie without risking my life. I had to admit I was relieved. My original plan to do this alone had terrified me.

'You should still be terrified,' Hannah said solemnly. 'You do realise this is going to be dangerous, even with the rest of us supporting you?'

For answer, I flung my arms round her and thanked her.

'I've always got your back,' she said. 'You know that. I just wish you'd trusted me from the start.'

'I wanted to, but I was afraid you'd convince me not to go ahead,' I admitted. 'I think I knew all along this was a risky plan. But with everyone on board, I'm sure we can pull it off. It's going to be fine, and we'll see Alfie behind bars before too long.'

'Are you trying to convince me, or yourself?' Hannah asked me.

'It's a good plan,' I insisted.

Poppy jumped out of her basket and came to join us again, wagging her tail and asking for attention.

'This part of the plan isn't for you, Poppy,' I said. 'You've done your bit, getting Sarah to meet me in the woods. Now it's over to me.'

Poppy gazed at me reproachfully before she turned away and trotted to her basket where she curled up with her back to me, studiously ignoring me.

18

THAT EVENING, POPPY AND I had an early supper before setting out for Hannah's house. It was a while since we had been there. We took a long way round to avoid walking along the whole length of the row of fairground vehicles, but we couldn't avoid going near them on our way to the bridge across the river. I kept my eyes fixed straight ahead, nervous in case we encountered Alfie before I had discussed the situation with my friends. Still undecided what to say to him, I was relieved when we left the encampment behind us and set foot on the bridge.

We passed a few people on our way over the river. A couple of them greeted me in passing, familiar faces from the tea shop, the pub, and Maud's grocery store, but we reached the far side of the river without meeting any of my friends. Had there been a different reason for my going to Hannah's house, I would have enjoyed the walk. The sun was still fairly high in the sky, but the heat of the day had passed and, following a light shower in the afternoon, the evening air smelled fresh and cool. Poppy frisked happily beside me, darting forward to chase a dragonfly that flitted out of her reach seconds before she caught it. Her jaws closed on empty air and she looked around in surprise.

Amused by her antics, I couldn't help smiling despite the gravity of my situation.

Adam and Hannah lived in a terraced red brick house on a new estate of similar properties, each of them small and neat, with tidy narrow front yards. Hannah opened the door and I complimented her on a vibrant bush growing in a large terracotta pot beside the front door. I commented on it whenever I went to visit her, and she always offered to give me a cutting. It had become a standing joke between us.

'One day we'll get round to it,' she promised me, and we both smiled, knowing it would probably never happen.

Fed up with waiting on the doorstep, Poppy tugged at her lead, eager to go inside where she knew she would get some attention. Adam was home, and Richard was there too, having arrived earlier as Hannah had invited him to join them for supper. As a schoolteacher, Toby finished work early and he was also there. Michelle had a shift at the pub, so we were just waiting for Barry before we began. I admitted that I hoped he wouldn't bring Samantha.

'It's not that I don't think we can trust her,' I added quickly. 'It's just that we hardly know her.'

Hannah looked surprised. 'Haven't you heard? Barry and Sam split up.'

'Really? They looked so happy together.'

'He's allergic to her cats.'

Poppy barked and wagged her tail, as if to say he ought to have enough sense to find a girlfriend with a dog.

'That's a pity,' I fibbed, doing my best to look sorry, although I was selfishly pleased.

Adam had opened a bottle of red wine, and Hannah offered us tea or coffee as an alternative.

'You can have both,' Hannah said.

'Tea and coffee?' Toby joked.

'If you like,' she replied, laughing, as she put a plate of fresh scones on the table. Anyone looking in would have seen a comfortable scene of domestic hospitality, with friends sitting around at a casual social gathering on a weekday evening. But some of us knew that there was a more ominous reason for our meeting. Poppy went straight over to Toby, who was the only one of us to have started on the scones.

'What's this all about, then?' he asked us, looking around as he petted Poppy. 'Sorry,' he added, mumbling through a mouthful, 'I'm starving. I haven't eaten yet. Michelle and I are going to have a curry later.'

Adam laughed. 'You don't need to make any excuses for wanting to tuck into Hannah's scones.'

Hannah disappeared into the kitchen, and we agreed to wait until she and Barry were with us before starting the meeting.

'Meeting?' Toby repeated, taking another scone. 'What meeting? What's going on?'

'There's milk and sugar on the table,' Hannah said, returning from the kitchen with a large cafetière of fresh coffee.

At last Barry arrived and we were all settled with cups of coffee, glasses of wine, and plates of pastries and scones. Poppy was in her element, circulating between us to hoover up crumbs and enjoy belly rubs and petting. I glanced at Barry who seemed slightly despondent, and wondered whether to say anything about Samantha but decided against it as no one else had mentioned her.

'Now,' Hannah said, sitting down. 'The floor's yours, Emily.'

Taking a deep breath, I launched into an account of Alfie's violent history, concluding with my scheme to record his confession. There was a stunned silence when I finished speaking.

'Are you sure about this?' Toby asked. Before I had a chance to defend my decision, he carried on. 'You're making a very serious accusation. I mean, murder has to be as bad as it gets. Granted someone must have killed that poor girl, how can you be sure it was this Alfie you keep talking about?'

Barry mumbled anxiously that the police had questioned Alfie, and had released him without charge. 'You might think he's guilty,' he added, 'but there's no evidence to support your accusation. You can't pin something on him just based on your opinion. I'm not saying you're wrong, but even with all their resources the police weren't able to prove anything against him. If you have evidence, take it to the police. Otherwise, you need to drop this.'

'There's no proof, as far as I know,' I replied. 'That's why we need him to confess.'

'Well, of course, an unforced confession would change things,' Barry conceded, looking sceptical. 'But I can't see that happening. We got nowhere when we questioned him.'

Not everyone agreed it would be sensible to try and press Alfie to confess.

'It's best to leave murder investigations to the police,' Barry insisted.

'For all you know, this Alfie could be innocent,' Toby pointed out, as he reached for another scone.

'He's not,' Richard said shortly, and everyone turned to look at him.

Richard repeated what Dana had told him about Alfie's assault on her. He had seen the scar on her arm, and he believed she had told him the truth about it. Astonished, Adam wanted to know when Richard had spoken to Dana, and why she had confided in him. When Richard admitted that Dana had been hiding out in his house, there was another stunned silence. Adam was clearly anxious, and Barry looked uncomfortable and said he wasn't sure he should be listening to the conversation.

'It's not a crime to put someone up,' I said, reminding them that Dana had stayed with me until Alfie found out where she was.

'And how did that work out for you?' Adam asked with barely concealed anger. 'Really, Dad, I can't believe you'd be so reckless, putting yourself at risk like this.'

'There's no risk, as long as no one else finds out where she is.'

Barry interrupted Adam's remonstrance to say we had no proof Alfie had been behind the vandalism at Rosecroft or the tea shop. He warned us not to get carried away by speculation.

'We haven't found any evidence,' he insisted.

'So what have the police been doing?' I demanded. 'Or should we all be like you and look the other way and pretend nothing's happened?'

'And there's the testimony from Dana's mother,' Richard added.

With a nod at him for the reminder, I related everything Sarah had told me, and finished by outlining her offer to install a camera in Alfie's caravan.

'It would be helpful to record him on video, not just audio,' Toby said. 'If you're sure Sarah's account is trustworthy. She could be covering up for her daughter, if she knows or suspects Dana's guilty. It sounds like Dana might have a motive for killing Alfie's new girlfriend.'

'What about her father?' I asked, furious that he was accusing Dana of murder. 'Are you going to tell us she might have killed him as well?'

Toby shrugged. 'Dana told you her father supported her when she wanted to leave Alfie, but what if her father was the one who opposed the marriage? He was the boss, wasn't he? Presumably he had the power to prevent Alfie marrying his daughter. Perhaps *she* was the one who wanted her father out of the way, or maybe she wanted revenge because he stopped her from marrying Alfie. I'm not saying I think that's true, only that it's possible.'

'Why would Sarah offer to set up a camera in Alfie's caravan, if she didn't think he was guilty?' I asked.

Barry nodded and muttered once again that we shouldn't jump to conclusions. Apart from Richard and me, everyone agreed Toby's theory was possible. But we all agreed there was nothing we could do to see Alfie arrested, unless we somehow forced a confession out of him. It was going to be a challenge to make that happen, and even more difficult to see how to do it without arousing his suspicion. Hannah pointed out, not for the first time, that if he really was a killer it might be extremely dangerous to try. Barry suggested we use a ring camera, so that he could be outside with Adam and Toby, watching what was happening inside Alfie's caravan. The discussion had undergone a subtle change of direction.

'The minute he lays a finger on you, we'll be in there,' Barry said, with uncharacteristic ferocity. 'But are you sure you know what you're doing? If he turns violent, he could attack in a second. You could be dead before we have a chance to break in.'

Sensitive to his tone, Poppy growled fiercely. When I reassured her that everything was all right, she rolled over and lay on her back, her legs waving in the air.

'I'm going to do this with or without your help,' I replied, petting her. 'Surely you can all see that I should at least try to trick Alfie into telling me what he did?' I asked. 'If he killed that poor girl, we can't just walk away and do nothing.'

Having expressed reservations about filming Alfie without his knowledge, even Barry had to agree that if my plan succeeded, Alfie would almost certainly be amenable to co-operating with the police.

'But why do *you* have to get involved?' Hannah asked me.

'Because I want to help Dana.'

My answer prompted a chorus of disapproval, with everyone saying it would be too risky. But no one was able to come up with any other ideas to establish the truth about Paris's death. Dana had agreed to show a picture of Sarah to Cliff so he could contact me and Barry the moment she entered the pub. It meant confiding in Cliff. I was slightly uneasy about the suggestion that we rely on yet more people, but at least it was a clear plan. In the absence of any better solution, that was what we decided to do.

No one seemed to approve of my plan, but I pointed out that if Alfie was innocent, he wouldn't implicate himself and there would be no harm done. Convinced that I was determined to go ahead, regardless of what anyone else said, Barry agreed to liaise with Dana so he could be waiting outside Alfie's caravan when I went in there. If he had to intervene, he could always claim he had just been passing when he heard shouting and went to investigate. We all agreed that was a good idea. Before we parted, we set up a group WhatsApp so we could keep in touch at all times. Barry refused to join the group and insisted we swear never to divulge his role in this underhanded process to anyone else. We all promised to be discreet. None of us wanted to get Barry in trouble.

'Are you sure you want to go ahead with this?' Barry asked me as we were leaving.

I nodded.

'You can change your mind at any time,' he added. 'If you decide to withdraw at the last minute, you can. Any time you feel unsure, just leave. If you're there with him, in his caravan, and you feel threatened, run. Make sure you don't let him get between you and the door, and remember we'll be right outside. Whatever happens, you won't be on your own in there.'

Poppy was trying to cling to my leg, as she did when she was tired, so I picked her up and thanked Barry for his support.

'You'd decided to go ahead with your scheme regardless, so you didn't leave me much choice,' he muttered, but I had the impression he was pleased to have an opportunity to help me.

He passed my road on his way back to his flat, so he accompanied me as far as the top of Mill Lane. We chatted about his aunt and her new husband, the butcher. Barry thought she might give up her shop soon, now she was married.

'It's getting a bit much for her,' he said. 'And she's not getting any younger.'

Having looked after Maud's shop for a fortnight while she and Norman were on their honeymoon, I agreed that running the shop was hard work.

We reached Mill Lane. Barry offered to walk up as far as Rosecroft with me, but I told him it wasn't necessary and he strode away before I had time to change my mind.

19

ALL THROUGH THE NEXT day, I kept my phone in my pocket and checked it regularly in case Cliff or Barry called me with any news. The thought that Sarah might walk into the pub at any time filled me with terror. Hannah didn't say anything, but I could sense her watching me whenever I moved into her line of vision. Like me, she was waiting. It didn't help my nerves that we were fairly quiet in the tea shop so I didn't even have many orders to distract me, and Poppy was at Jane's house with Lily. Time seemed to crawl really slowly without my receiving a message. We often had a lull in the early afternoon, between lunch and tea, and I was struggling not to think about Alfie, when my phone vibrated. Snatching it out of my pocket, I answered hastily without pausing to check the caller's name.

'That was quick,' my mother said.

'Oh, mum!'

Just in time, I restrained myself from blurting out that I was expecting to hear from someone else. That would inevitably have prompted awkward questions about who could be calling me at three in the afternoon.

What's going on, Emily? I could imagine her asking. *What is it you're keeping from me? Are you in trouble?*

I knew she meant well, but I really didn't want to discuss my plans with my mother, of all people. She would be understandably horrified by what I was intending to do. I wouldn't have put it past her to interfere, perhaps reporting my intentions to the police. Recovering from my surprise, I asked her how she was and she chattered about her art class, where the teacher had told her she showed real talent, and about my father's problematic feet. According to my mother, he was spending a fortune on a chiropodist who hadn't succeeded in making any discernible improvement to his ongoing issues.

'I mean, if we could see it was helping, I wouldn't begrudge a single penny of it, but we seem to be throwing money away. The chiropodist says it can take months to see any results, but in the meantime she's sitting there collecting his money and we won't know for ages whether the treatment is making any difference. So it's difficult to know what to do.'

After a minute or so I zoned out, grunting every now and again to indicate that I was paying attention, which I wasn't.

'Emily, are you listening to me, or am I talking to myself?' my mother demanded after a few minutes.

I assured her that she had my full attention, and soon after that a customer came in. Promising to call her back later, I rang off, relieved.

Hannah and I arranged to meet in the pub after supper. In the meantime life had to continue as normal. After feeding Poppy that evening, I set out. It was raining, and Poppy hated getting wet, so I picked her up and, sheltering her under my coat, hurried to The Plough. My coat was reasonably waterproof but the hems of my trouser legs were uncomfortably damp by the time we arrived. A small group from the fairground was seated at a table nearest the door. I glanced at them in passing, and immediately dropped my eyes before any of them noticed me looking at them, but I had seen enough to ascertain that neither Alfie nor Sarah was among them. Hannah and Adam were seated in another corner and Poppy joined them, while I went to get a drink.

My friends and I sat in silence for a moment. Only Poppy appeared to be completely at ease, moving from one to another of us soliciting attention. All I could think about was my proposed meeting with Sarah, which none of us could mention in case we were overheard. Barry was not there, but I hardly dared to speculate about whether he might have visited the fairground camp that day. In a way I hoped he had, as I was feeling increasingly nervous about going ahead with the plan. Despite the fact that I had persuaded my friends to agree to it, if we didn't act soon I would probably end up backing out altogether. The more I thought about it, the more foolhardy it all seemed. Recalling how Hannah and my mother had both recently criticised me for being rash reminded me of my promise to call my mother that evening. I was about to take out my phone when Hannah fixed her eyes on me with a curious intensity, as though she wanted to attract my attention.

'What's up?' I asked her.

'Is that her?' Adam hissed.

'Don't look round,' Hannah added urgently before I could turn my head.

The door was behind me, but I gathered that Sarah had just walked in. Cliff approached our table and nodded at me, confirming my suspicion. My heart seemed to race in my chest; the camera had been installed in Alfie's caravan. Now I just had to find him, and make sure my friends were there if I needed help.

'Half an hour,' I said quietly.

I texted Barry, using the cryptic code we had agreed on earlier. 'RUOK?' He responded almost immediately, 'OK'. Afraid that Barry could lose his job if it ever came out that he had been instrumental in helping us to covertly film Alfie, we kept our messages vague. It was probably illegal to film Alfie without his permission, and definitely inappropriate for Barry to be complicit in an attempt to entrap a suspect. Feeling nervous, I went to the loo and sat in a cubicle, shaking, and wondering what on earth I was doing. If I hadn't been stupid enough to tell all my friends about my plan, I could have changed my mind. As it was, I felt obliged to at least try to implement the plan. The more I thought about it, the crazier it seemed, but there was no going back now.

Returning to the bar, I sat down and checked the time. It was ten past ten. In twenty minutes I could be in Alfie's caravan, plying him with alcohol, and encouraging him to tell me everything about himself. I said goodbye to Hannah and Adam and then, armed with a bottle of whisky from Cliff, and with Poppy trotting beside me, I set off to look for Alfie. With any luck, he would spot me and invite me in without my having to do much searching. And if I was even luckier, I would be unable to find him at all. The moon was out and it was a still night. A light shower had fallen earlier, and the grass was damp, but the rain had stopped. Under normal circumstances, Poppy and I would have enjoyed our walk. As it was, she seemed to sense my anxiety. Instead of darting around, sniffing everywhere, she stayed close to me. As we approached the line of caravans and trailers, she whimpered softly. Finally she sat down, refusing to continue. I had no choice but to pick her up and walk on with her in my arms, not really sure where I was going. The encampment seemed deserted, with no noise coming from any of the caravans. Finally, I saw a boy seated on the steps of a trailer, whittling a piece of wood. He had a mop of auburn curls, and I judged him to be about ten or eleven. Going over to him, I asked him if he knew where Alfie lived. The boy stopped scraping his piece of wood and twisted his neck to look up at me with a diffident air. He kept silent, so I repeated my enquiry. This time, the boy turned his head and spat on the ground.

'If you could just point me in the right direction,' I said. 'Then I'll take it from there.'

I put Poppy down and she trotted forwards, wagging her tail in a friendly overture. The boy carefully put his knife down and stood up.

'That dog didn't ought to be here,' he told me. 'You're trespassing, and so is your dog.'

'This is public land,' I replied. 'It doesn't belong to you.' Impatiently, I repeated my request for him to point out where Alfie lived.

'Alfie?' he echoed, sullenly scraping a muddy trainer through the damp grass.

'Yes, Alfie,' I replied, trying to maintain calm.

With a shrug, he sat back down on the steps and resumed whittling his stick, appearing to have forgotten all about me. Poppy started barking and the door of the trailer creaked open behind the boy.

'What's going on out there?' a shrill voice called out. 'Is that you, Billy? What's all that racket?'

'She's asking for Alfie,' the boy replied, putting his knife down again and pointing his finger at me. 'She wants to know where he lives.'

'What's it to you?' the woman asked, moving onto the top of the steps and staring down at me.

Tall and broad, she stood with her hands on her hips, studying me as though sizing me up before launching herself down the steps, her long crimson hair streaming down her back. My naturally red mop was unremarkable compared to her dazzling mane which couldn't have been natural. She glared at me with strange intensity. Had Poppy not been standing beside me, wagging her tail excitedly, I might have turned and fled. As it was, I could feel my legs shaking.

'I'm looking for Alfie.' Forcing myself to smile, I explained that Alfie had invited me to his caravan, adding that I didn't know where to find him.

'Oh, Alfie invited you to his caravan, did he?' The woman sniffed. 'Invited you to his caravan? And what's Lizzie going to say about that?' She shook her head and gazed at me with a pitying expression.

'I haven't spoken to anyone called Lizzie,' I replied, looking up at her with what I hoped was a disarming smile. 'Alfie invited me to his caravan so I thought I'd pay him a visit, that's all. Can you tell me which caravan is his?'

'Oh, go home, you simpleton. Alfie's not for the likes of you,' she said impatiently.

'Simpleton,' the boy sniggered.

'You be quiet, Billy. Where are your manners?' the woman snapped at him. Turning back to me, she lowered her voice and glanced around as though worried she might be overheard. 'You look like a respectable girl. Why do you want to get mixed up with the likes of Alfie? He won't do you no good.' She lowered her voice even further, until she was speaking in a barely audible whisper. 'You'll get off home sharpish, if you know what's good for you.'

There was no point in continuing the conversation, so I spun round and stalked away, with Poppy scampering beside me. The boy returned to his whittling and the woman went back inside her trailer, muttering, and slamming her door behind her. This was not the welcome I had expected, and finding Alfie was supposed to be the straightforward part of my mission. It would have been easy to give up at that stage, but far from being put off by the woman's warning, I was more determined than ever to stick to my plan. Sarah had planted the camera in readiness, and I would be letting everyone down if I walked away now. I had expected persuading Alfie to confide in me would be my biggest challenge but, so far, I hadn't even been able to find him.

From what I had heard about Alfie, I guessed he would position himself somewhere near the centre of the camp, so that was where I decided to begin my search.

'Come on, Poppy,' I urged her, dragging her through a gap between two trailers and stepping carefully over a thick black cable. 'Let's go and find him.'

The moon was bright and we walked carefully through shadows cast by the fairground vehicles. Somewhere nearby a dog let out a deep throated bark, and I wondered if it was Sarah's Alsatian. Poppy yapped excitedly in response.

'Hello,' a voice said suddenly, making me jump. 'Who do we have here, making an unholy din and disturbing the peace?'

Startled and quite scared, I turned and saw Alfie leaning against the side of a dark trailer, grinning at me. With a tight white T-shirt showing off his athletic physique, in the semi-darkness he looked every inch a romantic hero. Poppy began barking earnestly, and Alfie spun round to frown at her. I wondered if it had been a blunder to bring her with me, but it was too late to change my mind. For a fleeting instant, I felt an overwhelming wave of relief, thinking that Alfie would not want me to go back to his caravan with him after all, since I had brought Poppy with me. Then he turned his gaze on me, his eyes gleaming in the moonlight.

'Looking for me?' he purred. 'Well, you've found me,' he went on in a husky voice, without waiting for my answer. 'Come on. This way.'

A quotation from Shakespeare flashed into my mind. We had studied Henry V at school, and I recalled the concluding words of a famous speech: "The game's afoot!". Of course, Shakespeare had nothing to do with my mission to record Alfie, but the game was most certainly afoot.

20

ALFIE LED ME PAST a row of trailers to the centre of the encampment, where we threaded our way through a maze of haphazardly parked caravans. Mostly white, they were difficult to tell apart. Some looked cleaner than others, but all were splashed with mud after the recent rain. Poppy whimpered as we followed our guide, who picked his way between them with ease, and I couldn't help admiring how surefooted he was as I stumbled over cables and random logs. Some of the caravans had stripes painted along their sides, thin lines of red, blue and green, and coloured curtains hanging at the windows, in an attempt to individualise them and brighten them up. Finding the way around them was probably easy for a member of the community like Alfie, who would recognise each individual vehicle and its curtains, and be familiar with all of the people living in them, but it would have been challenging for me to find my way around this labyrinth on my own.

Only faintly noticeable from a distance, a variety of sounds and smells now assailed us more strongly: a muffled cacophony of voices, calling out and chattering, quarrelling and laughing and singing; and aromas of bacon, onions, sausages, curry, beer, and a scent of something sweet and sugary. These were the mobile homes where the fairground community lived.

'Where are we going?' I asked. Hurrying to keep up with Alfie, I nearly tripped over a cable hidden in shadow between two vehicles.

'It's not much further,' he called out over his shoulder, without turning round.

At last he stopped by a dilapidated caravan parked by the river some distance from the others. Approaching, I saw that the door and window frames were rusty and the sides were dented and scratched. Something, perhaps a collision with another vehicle, had gouged a long groove along one side of the front section of the caravan, damage which no one had tried to repair. It formed an ugly slash of rust, like a bloody wound in the dirty white paintwork.

I shivered in the gathering darkness. Poppy whimpered and pressed her trembling body against my leg.

'Here we are,' Alfie said cheerfully, peering all around as though checking no one was watching us.

He took a key out of his pocket and unlocked the door, which creaked open with a rasping sound that wouldn't have been out of place in a horror film. Through the open door I caught a glimpse of a grubby floor and a bench covered in worn and ripped leather. Reaching out to seize me by the elbow, Alfie steered me towards it. Poppy let out a fierce bark. Reminded of my little companion, Alfie scowled.

'You can leave the mutt outside,' he muttered, adding that he liked to keep his caravan clean.

'Poppy won't make a mess,' I assured him, without commenting on the filthy state of the vehicle. 'She's well trained.'

'I want to spend time with you on your own,' he murmured in my ear.

Realising that tying Poppy up outside would make it easy for my friends to find me, I crouched down and attached her lead to the hitch at the front of the caravan. She whimpered miserably, making me feel terrible, but it had to be done. Alfie watched me with a complacent grin.

'Just wait here,' I whispered to her. 'Wait. I'll be back soon.' I hoped that was true.

There was no sign of my friends, and I was pleased they had concealed themselves so effectively. They would be listening to Poppy's frantic whimpering, and doubtless observing me while taking care not to betray their presence.

Looking around, I repeated the instruction to wait. 'And no barking,' I added sternly. 'We don't want to disturb anyone.'

Poppy obediently stopped whimpering and lay down. Resting her chin on her front paws, she gazed mournfully up at me but was silent. I turned back to Alfie who was waiting for me by the open door.

'Come on,' he called out impatiently.

'Wait here, Poppy,' I repeated my instruction, raising my voice for my friends' benefit. 'I'm going into the caravan with Alfie now.'

Stifling my apprehension, I entered the dirty caravan and Alfie followed me. To my dismay, he turned the key in the door behind him.

'Why did you lock the door?'

'We don't want to be interrupted, do we?' he replied.

Seeing his leering face, I shuddered inwardly, wondering how I had ever thought he was attractive. Reminding myself that my friends were waiting outside, I did my best to control my nerves, telling myself that they would have little difficulty in breaking down the door on such a rusty old caravan. Meanwhile, I needed to focus my attention on my immediate situation. Inside, the caravan was dark and it smelled dank and musty. On the left of the door, a square bed took up one end of the interior. There were no sheets or pillows, only a grubby blue mattress on a base that tilted to one side. A tattered brown leather sofa was fixed to one wall of a kitchen area which consisted of a worktop, once white but now speckled with grey mould, and a sink surrounded by what looked like some kind of greenish slime. A few dirty plates lay piled up beside the sink, along with a chipped glass vase. There were no flowers in it, but a scummy green line was visible on the inside, where it had once held water.

Other than that, there were a few drawers and cupboards and a space where an oven or a fridge might have stood. There was no food to be seen, but that would probably have been rotten and only added to the general stench of mould and decay. Looking to the right, I saw a stained yellow formica table and two plastic benches, all fixed to the floor. The whole place looked as though it hadn't been cleaned for months, if not years. Cautiously I sat down on one of the benches and stifled a cry of disgust when my fingers brushed against the sticky table top.

Surreptitiously wiping my hand on my jeans, I looked all around, but there was no sign of a camera anywhere. Sarah had hidden it well. I wondered fleetingly whether Alfie had discovered it and removed it, but there was nothing in his demeanour to suggest he was suspicious of me.

'Is this where you live?' I asked him, gazing around uncomfortably.

His warm smile was somehow menacing. Close up, his white T-shirt looked grubby and I caught a whiff of cologne and sweat.

'Come over here, gorgeous,' he said softly, sitting on the edge of the mattress.

I stared at it in disgust, half expecting to see bed bugs or other crawling creatures wriggle out of it as it sank under his weight. My legs trembled as I rose from the bench and took a step towards him. As I moved, my bag shifted on my shoulder. Recalling the plan I had devised with my friends, I opened my bag and drew out the bottle of whisky Cliff had given me.

'I brought this,' I said, smiling uneasily and holding it up so he could see it.

Alfie leaped to his feet and grabbed the bottle from me. 'Nice one,' he said. 'This'll do to start with.'

He raised the bottle to his lips and gulped noisily. When he held the bottle out to me, I saw that he must have downed nearly a quarter of it. Thoughts whirled crazily through my mind as I made a pretence of drinking, hoping that the alcohol would kill any germs his lips had left on the bottle. The plan had been to get him drunk so he would be more likely to talk freely. Hopefully he would also be easier to overpower if he attempted to kiss me but, with any luck, he would fall asleep before that. On the other hand, it struck me that he might lose all self-control and become violent. Alone with Alfie, I felt vulnerable, and had to remind myself that my friends would burst in if he threatened to become aggressive. I was ready to scream if necessary. Feeling a little safer clutching a bottle as a potential weapon, I returned it to him reluctantly when he reached for it. If I aroused his suspicion, the whole plan would be ruined.

'Pretty decent,' he said, wiping his lips on the back of his hand, when he had swigged some more.

He was still sitting upright, but his speech was now slightly slurred. I inched away from him along the bench, keeping one eye on the locked door, and cursing under my breath because the key was in Alfie's pocket.

'Come and sit down,' he called to me, waving the bottle of whisky in the air and grinning. 'Come on, darling, don't be shy. I'm not going to eat you.' He laughed as though he had cracked a joke, and swayed slightly.

'Are you hungry?' I blurted out, to avoid joining him on the mattress. 'Let's have something to eat. I'm starving. Is there anything here?'

Searching the kitchen cupboards, I found only a rusty old kettle and a block of stale cheese, hard as a brick. The shelves were greasy and grey with a film of filth, and there was a smell of rotting cabbage.

'What a pity for you to live like this, all by yourself,' I said, searching for a way to steer the conversation towards his dead girlfriend and coax a confession from him as quickly as possible. 'This place stinks. I suppose you live here all alone now, with no one to help you with the cooking and cleaning? You were living with Paris, weren't you? You must miss her terribly.' I heaved a fake sigh. 'It must be very hard for you, losing her so suddenly.'

Alfie took another swig of whisky and held the bottle out to me.

'Here,' he said. 'Have a drink and stop fussing.'

'But you must miss Paris,' I hazarded, hoping I wasn't betraying my interest in her too blatantly.

Alfie shrugged. 'She's dead and gone.' He waved the bottle in the air again. 'She's history. Don't give her another thought. What is all this?' He stared at me and I held my breath, wondering if I had pushed my agenda too far, and whether I ought to start screaming. 'Come on now, get over here. Don't be shy.'

I sat back down on the mucky bench. 'You must miss her very much,' I persisted, determined to keep the table between us and persuade him to talk about his dead girlfriend.

'Miss who?' he asked, his words running into each other.

'We're talking about Paris.'

'Paris is dead,' he repeated, with a shrug. 'She won't be coming back. I told you, she's history.' He waved his hand in a dismissive gesture. 'You don't need to worry about her. She won't be disturbing us. No one will.'

'But you lived together, didn't you?' I persevered, trying to sound casual. The conversation was not going the way I had planned. 'It must be difficult for you to carry on living here without her. Maybe I could help you make it nice again?' I added, with a flash of inspiration.

I was prepared to roll my sleeves up and do some cleaning, anything to avoid lying down on the filthy mattress with Alfie. While we were talking, it struck me that so much dirt couldn't possibly have accumulated in the caravan in the short time that had elapsed since the murder, and a sudden chill struck me.

'You do you live here, don't you?' I asked him.

'Sure. Me and my people, we all live here,' he replied, falling back on the mattress and closing his eyes.

Feeling increasingly uncomfortable, trapped in a cramped space with a suspected killer who wanted to have sex with me, I was overwhelmed by a desperate urge to escape from that foul-smelling caravan. If the door hadn't been locked, I would probably have abandoned the plan and made a break for it right then. No one would have blamed me. It was a harebrained scheme anyway. Alfie was lying down, with his eyes closed. If I moved swiftly, I could have been out of the caravan before he realised what was happening. But I was trapped by the locked door. In any case, I had gone there to persuade Alfie to incriminate himself on camera, and it would be spineless to surrender to panic and leave without at least attempting to complete my mission. It had to be possible to persuade him to talk. I couldn't believe he had no feelings at all about Paris. On an impulse, I decided to take the plunge and ask him directly what had happened to her.

I held my breath, waiting for his answer.

'What happened to Paris?' he repeated slowly, raising himself onto one elbow. 'Stupid cow went and got herself killed. Don't you know anything? Everyone knows what happened to Paris. Caused us no end of trouble. The police were here, talking to everyone.' He leaned forward and spat on the floor. 'Now, are you going to come here, or do I have to drag you? Is that what you're waiting for?' He grinned and licked his lips. 'Like a bit of rough, do you?'

'I'm not sure it's such a good idea,' I blurted out in alarm. Seeing his expression darken, I added quickly, 'I mean, doing anything here. You have a reputation to think of among your people. You know how they all admire you.' I wasn't quite sure what I was talking about, but he was too drunk to realise I was gabbling nonsense.

'Don't worry,' he replied. 'I can do what I want. Anyway, no one's going to disturb us here. You just lie back and enjoy it. We won't be interrupted. So, come on, it's time to have some fun. That is what you're after, isn't it?'

'No,' I blurted out. 'That is, not yet.'

'Playing hard to get, are you?' He sneered. 'Come on, cut the act. We both know why you're here. Why else did you come looking for me?'

'I wasn't looking for you,' I protested. 'I was taking my dog for a walk.' Remembering the reason I was there, I pulled myself up short and resumed my efforts to encourage him to talk.

What made my situation really precarious was that he was bound to be furious when he realised he wasn't going to get what he wanted from me. Pillow talk was all well and good, but I had no intention of going to bed with Alfie. All I could think of was that I had to find a way to persuade him to talk to me without letting him touch me. It was hard to see how I was going to manage that. Outside, all was quiet as my friends watched on Hannah's phone and waited for him to confess. Even Poppy was silent. Obedient to my command, she hadn't barked once, and had probably fallen asleep. Frantically I wracked my brains to come up with a strategy to make Alfie confess, but my situation seemed hopeless.

21

STILL SITTING ON THE bench, I glanced over at Alfie who looked half asleep. It seemed I was never going to persuade him to confide in me, and soon it would be too dark for the camera to video his face. Just as I decided it was time to give up and find a way to leave, Alfie reached out with one hand and a dim light came on beside the bed. With half of his face lit up, and the other side masked in shadow, he looked quite demonic, but it was a relief to know that if he did say something to incriminate himself, at least his face would be visible on the video recording.

'What's the matter with you?' he asked, his head lolling to one side, away from the light. 'Why are you still sitting at the table, instead of coming over here? You know you didn't come here for something to eat. Come on, there's plenty of room.'

He thumped the mattress more vigorously than before, sending particles of dust floating through the faint glow cast by the light.

'Don't you think we ought to talk first?' I suggested.

'What for?'

'To get to know one another, before we take things any further.'

'What is there to talk about? Get over here.' He took another swig of whisky and fell back on the mattress again, laughing. 'I'll show you how we can get to know one another better. Come on, let's see more of each other right now. There's no need to be coy with me. Come on, have a drink and get out of those clothes. Enjoy yourself. Let your hair down. You're so stiff, one of these days you're going to snap in half. It's no good for you, being so uptight,' he went on in a wheedling tone. 'You need to relax, and this will help you. Come on, stop wasting time. There's playing hard to get and there's being downright annoying.'

Lying flat on the bed, he held the bottle up in the air and, this time, I saw that nearly half of the whisky had gone. Convinced he couldn't remain conscious for much longer, I determined to keep him away from me until he passed out. Already his eyes were beginning to glaze over and his speech was sounding increasingly garbled.

'I can see you're upset about what happened to Paris,' I said tentatively, 'and really, who can blame you?'

'What do you mean? Why would anyone blame *me*?' he asked, his voice suddenly sharp.

I waited, crossing my fingers, but he lay still and didn't say anything else.

'Alfie?' I called out softly. 'Are you awake?'

Partly relieved, but at the same time disappointed at having failed in my task, I thought he had fallen asleep. I was considering giving up when he startled me by sitting up suddenly.

'What's that supposed to mean?' he demanded sharply. His speech was slurred but his feelings were clear.

His ferocity took me aback but, at the same time, I was excited because it seemed that he might finally be ready to open up about the murder. I glanced around, even though I knew the camera was too well hidden to be seen. Sarah had done well.

'I'm talking about Paris,' I said patiently. 'As her boyfriend, you must have felt you should have been able to look after her. But you can't blame yourself. It wasn't your fault she had a fatal accident when you weren't on hand to save her. You weren't to know what was going to happen. I only meant that I feel sorry for you, that's all. Everyone does. After all, you must have cared about her. You were living together, weren't you?'

The angry flush faded from his cheeks and he fell back on the bed again, muttering that he didn't want to talk about his former girlfriend, and he hadn't realised I was so boring.

'I thought you would be more fun than this,' he complained, and closed his eyes.

All at once, he grunted irritably and sat up. 'This has gone on long enough,' he said. 'You're boring me. I don't know what stupid game you think you're playing, but it's not funny. Now let's do what we came here to do. Take your clothes off and come over here.'

I pressed on frantically, determined not to be deflected from my purpose.

'Tell me about Paris,' I repeated.

'You keep going on about Paris,' he complained. 'Paris, Paris, Paris. The stupid cow was a waste of space. I had to get rid of her.'

'Get rid of her?' I repeated, hardly daring to breathe.

'She was a looker, all right, but stupid. Girls like her are easy to come by, sluts the lot of them, and she was getting in my way. So I sent her packing.' I gasped. He sat up, leaning shakily on one elbow and lowered his voice conspiratorially. 'When I heard she was dead, I knew she'd topped herself because I'd thrown her over. But no, the police said it must be murder and they hounded me about it. Ex-boyfriend, had to be guilty. Idiots.'

I stifled a sigh, disappointed that he wasn't confessing to having killed her. I nearly pointed out that he had tried to convince me that Dana had murdered Paris, so he knew she hadn't killed herself, but he carried on.

'She was a looker, I'll give her that. Look,' he went on. 'Since you're so interested in her, come here and I'll show you some photos of her.' He held out his phone, but I hesitated. 'All right,' he conceded, 'I'll come over there.'

He pulled himself off the mattress, grumbling, and staggered over to sit down heavily on the opposite side of the table to me. I wasn't sure whether to be pleased that he hadn't come to sit beside me, or anxious because he had positioned himself between me and the door, blocking my escape route. He took out his phone and held it up.

'That's a nice phone,' I said.

He nodded. 'Latest one. What have you got?'

I took my phone from my pocket and he held out a calloused hand for it. 'You show me yours and I'll show you mine,' he said, giggling like a schoolgirl.

Amazed that he was capable of conversing after drinking so much, I gave him my phone and he made a show of studying it.

'Not bad,' he said. 'Not bad. Now, you were asking about Paris,' he went on, and I nodded. 'It wasn't murder at all, no matter what anyone tells you. The police wanted to use her death to persecute me. That's how they work. And it's not just the police. You might not believe it, but there are people here who are out to get me. Jealous, the lot of them. Fancy they're better than me.' He turned his head aside and spat on the floor.

'So you think it was an accident?' I said, doing my best to hide my disappointment.

He shook his head. 'I never said that. No, she topped herself after I dumped her, and that's all I'm going to say. But you won't be so stupid. I can see you're just up for a good time. Best way. The only way, if you ask me. Don't go making any demands, because I won't have it.' He swayed slightly on the bench and his eyes began to close.

It was time to abandon my mission, and I made a snap decision. 'I don't want to be here any longer,' I announced abruptly. 'I'm leaving.'

Opening glazed eyes, Alfie looked around groggily. 'You don't have to be frightened of me, you know. I'm not going to hurt you. And I won't try and force you to do anything you don't want to do. We can just talk, for a while, if that's what you want. What the hell's the matter with you anyway? Is this about Lizzie? You don't want to worry about her. Come on, we're already friends.' He paused as though struggling to think. 'We can be more than friends. You want that, don't you? I know that's what you came here for.' He nodded. 'You can't pull the wool over my eyes. I know what you want. Forget about Lizzie. She's nothing.'

'I don't know anything about Lizzie, or anyone else, and I don't want to know,' I snapped. 'I just want to go home. Unlock the door and let me go, now, or you'll be sorry.'

He didn't yet know that we were being observed.

'No need to get in a strop about it. There's no cause for you to be jealous. Anyway, I thought you wanted to talk.'

I took a deep breath, aware that I was flirting, not with Alfie, but with danger. But a chance to persuade him to talk had unexpectedly presented itself, and it was too good an opportunity to miss.

'Tell me about Paris,' I said.

He stood up unsteadily, and glared at me.

'Why are you so obsessed with Paris? She's dead and gone. History.'

'I'm concerned about you,' I said. 'Everyone is.'

'Everyone needs to mind their own bloody business,' he muttered, sitting down again abruptly. 'What's it got to do with you? I told you, she topped herself.'

'I need to know that you're all right,' I lied desperately. 'If we're going to do anything, like have any sort of relationship, I want to know that you're not just on the rebound. How are you coping with losing Paris so suddenly? It must have been horrible for you. You're still grieving and you need to give yourself time to process what happened. It was very sudden, wasn't it? And you were living together, weren't you? You must need to talk to someone about what happened. It might be difficult to open up to your friends and neighbours, but I'm an outsider and you can talk freely to me. This will all be in confidence. I just want to help you.' I was aware that I was repeating myself, clutching at straws, but he was too drunk to take in what I was saying.

Alfie grunted and muttered about finding my presence tedious.

'So you used to live here with Paris?' I pressed on, doggedly sticking to my purpose. 'I mean, here, in this actual caravan. How long did you live with her, here?'

Alfie burst out laughing. 'Here?' he spluttered. 'Me? Alfie Cooper live here? You're taking the piss. You don't seriously think I would live in this old heap of rust? Hardly.' He laughed again.

I stared at him, aghast. For a moment I was too shocked to respond.

At last I croaked in a strangled voice, 'Why did you bring me here?'

'For the same reason that you came looking for me,' he answered impatiently.

'Why didn't we go to the caravan where you live?'

'Not a good idea to take you to my place just now,' he replied breezily. 'Not while Lizzie's there. She might kick off. She can be difficult when she's in one of her moods, and we don't want her spoiling our fun, do we?'

'Lizzie?' I repeated. 'What has she got to do with us?' I asked, although I realised what he meant.

'She's my girlfriend, or she thinks she is anyway. Don't look so disappointed,' he added. 'You play your cards right and she won't be around for much longer.' He laughed and winked at me. 'If she's not careful, she'll be following Paris soon.'

'What do you mean?' I asked, and he laughed again.

'Don't you worry about Lizzie,' he said, waving the bottle at me. 'Come over to the bed with me and have a drink. It's time we got to know one another properly. Jesus, you've been here jawing half the night, and I'm done with the chat. Get yourself over there, or do I have to drag you with me to the bed?'

'Do you mean this isn't your caravan?' I managed to stammer. 'But did you ever live here, in this caravan? Did you live here with Paris?'

'In this old rust bucket? Hardly. No, this caravan belonged to old Mathew, but he's gone to a better place, bless him. He died right there,' he added, pointing to the bed. 'This caravan's been empty for a while, and I've got the only key. Bit of luck for us, eh? No one's going to come looking for us here.'

I stared at him, too shocked to respond. My friends were watching the wrong caravan, and I was all alone with a vicious misogynist who was almost certainly a killer.

'It's late,' I said, standing up. 'It's time I left. You need to get some sleep, and I don't want to stay here all night. Someone might see me leaving in the morning. Open the door and I'll be off.'

'Oh, very well,' he said, also standing up and appearing to reach a decision. 'It was a waste of time bringing you here. I thought you'd be more fun than this.'

Evidently he had accepted that I wasn't going to sleep with him, just as I had realised he was never going to confide any guilty secrets to me. In any case, now that it was clear our conversation was not being recorded, there was no longer much point in trying to persuade him to confide in me. My word against his in a court of law wasn't likely to hold much weight. He could be very persuasive and charming, when he wasn't intoxicated, and my testimony would almost certainly be dismissed as vexatious, coming from a woman he had rejected. I would be characterised as jealous and malicious, and even my friends would despise me.

'Pity,' Alfie muttered, rising to his feet. I walked round the table and was right behind him when he reached the door. Instead of opening it, he spun round and slammed me in the stomach with the whisky bottle. Caught unawares and winded, I stumbled backwards and almost fell, banging my hip painfully against the corner of the table.

'No one turns me down,' he snarled. 'Paris thought she could leave me, but I made sure she never had the chance to get away.'

'What do you mean?' I gasped, moving back behind the table in alarm.

'She got what she deserved. I made sure of that,' he replied. 'That's made you think twice about turning me down, hasn't it?' He grinned.

'Are you saying you killed her?' I repeated, too horrified by his casual confession to consider my own peril.

'The stupid cow brought it on herself. And you'd better sort out your attitude if you don't want to go the same way.'

Having issued that threat, he flung open the door and leaped outside, slamming it shut before I could reach it. As I lunged forward, I heard the scraping of his key in the lock. I grabbed the door handle and twisted it, shaking it violently, but to no avail. The door didn't budge. In a panic, I felt in my pocket for my phone, but it wasn't there. Having emptied out my bag on the table, I dropped to my hands and knees. As I searched the floor, I remembered swapping phones with Alfie. I recalled putting his down on the table after looking at it, but couldn't remember him returning my phone to me. He must have been planning, even then, to leave me in the caravan alone, unable to summon help.

I shook the door handle and called out, but no one answered. Probably no one could hear me. I wondered what had happened to Poppy, and if I would ever see her again. Overcome with self-pity and anger at my own stupidity I began to cry. Knowing that my friends were watching and waiting outside a different caravan made my situation even more galling. When they saw no sign that I needed help, they would probably abandon their vigil, thinking I had given up and gone home.

After a few moments, I pulled myself together and began looking around for a means of escape. I called to Poppy, but there was no response.

'Poppy, wake up!' I yelled. 'Find Hannah! Poppy!'

There was no answering bark, not even a whimper. Terrified that Alfie might have harmed Poppy, I returned to the door and jiggled the handle frantically, again and again, but the door remained securely shut. Even if I had the tools necessary for picking a lock, I would have no idea what to do with them. Frustrated, I tried the handle again, but still nothing happened. The door didn't even shake in its rusty frame. For all that the caravan was old and rickety, it was solidly constructed. I tried once again, but it made no difference. The door didn't even judder. Outside, it was now completely dark and no lights were visible through the dirt-smeared windows.

Somehow I had to escape. Fetching the lamp so I could study the door more closely, I noticed it was quite heavy. Clambering onto the grubby sofa, I swung the base of the lamp at the window, but it didn't even make a dent. The window appeared to be made of some kind of plastic or perspex, not glass, and I succeeded only in making my shoulder ache. The windows were unbreakable, and the door locked. In desperation, I began beating out a rhythm on the side of the caravan with the base of the lamp: three bangs in quick succession followed by three bangs at slightly longer intervals and finally three rapid bangs again. I hoped that was the correct sequence for SOS in morse code, although I wasn't sure if the signal started with three short sounds or three long sounds. Either way, my cell was isolated from the other caravans, and it seemed unlikely that anyone would hear me.

I had voluntarily walked into a trap with no means of escape. No one else was aware of my predicament and, for all I knew, Alfie was prepared to leave me there to die. He had been so drunk when he had incarcerated me, he might not even remember I was there. As a psychopath, I certainly wouldn't care. It was no comfort to know that, having deliberately and willingly orchestrated the situation myself, I had only myself to blame for my predicament.

'Poppy,' I called out hopelessly. 'Poppy, where are you?'

22

IT WAS DARK OUTSIDE, and impossible to see much inside the caravan by the dim light of the lamp. There would be little point in trying to attract attention from across the river, as anyone walking there would be too far away to hear me. One side of the caravan faced towards the rest of the vehicles, where there was a chance someone might notice my banging, but I couldn't remember which side that was. With no lights to guide me, I kept thumping on the door and each of the walls in turn, hoping one of them pointed in the right direction. By now I had spent a few hours in the foul-smelling caravan, but it felt like longer. My mouth was dry and my head ached, possibly from dehydration.

Checking the sink, I found there was running water, but there was no way of knowing whether it was safe to drink. There was a rusty old travelling kettle, barely large enough to hold two cups of water and, although I had nothing to drink from, this was better than nothing. On balance, I decided to boil the water and was ridiculously pleased to find the kettle worked when I plugged it in. I rinsed it out several times, to remove the worst of the rust and dust. After several minutes, I had a small kettle's worth of discoloured water. It was too hot for now, but I had only to wait for it to cool down and I would be able to have a drink. Searching through the cupboards, I came across an unopened can of coca cola in a drawer beside the bed. Wiping the dust from the top, I drank it greedily. Once that was gone, I had only rusty boiled water to drink and nothing to eat. Feeling revived, at least temporarily, I realised it was too dangerous to sit around waiting to be rescued. Before anyone else could find me, my captor might come back. I had to escape before that happened.

If Alfie returned, it might be possible to knock him out with the lamp, but I wasn't confident I could do that. I had never hit anyone in my life and wasn't sure I would have the strength to overpower a strong man, even if my life was at stake. I considered waiting behind the door and throwing myself out of the caravan as soon as it opened, but I had no idea when – or even if – Alfie was planning to return. Possibly he had been spooked by my harping on about Paris, and had decided to leave me to rot in that stinking abandoned caravan. I imagined someone coming across my corpse after months, or perhaps years. The smell would probably be the first thing to alert anyone passing to the presence of a cadaver inside the caravan. Before that happened, Alfie might return to dispose of me. I pictured him throwing my body in the river, weighted down with rocks. My remains would sink to the bottom and slowly decompose, never to be found again.

My most miserable reverie revolved around Poppy, and what would happen to her. I wondered if she was still tied to the caravan, and hoped someone would find her soon. Alfie had probably released her as her presence was bound to attract suspicion, especially once my friends started to search for me. In the morning, Hannah would notice I hadn't turned up for work, and my friends would discover I wasn't at home. I imagined Alfie asking his new girlfriend, Lizzie, to answer my phone and impersonate me if anyone called.

I'm fine, I imagined her saying, holding her nose to disguise her voice, and telling Hannah that she had contracted a contagious disease. *I'm feeling rotten so I've gone away to rest and recover. Sorry for dropping you in it, but I didn't want to see you and pass on my germs. I may be off work for some time. You won't be able to find me, but don't worry. I'll be okay. It's best if you just forget about me.* Of course, Hannah would never fall for a stunt like that, and would initiate a hunt for me straightaway. Only by then, I might be feeding the fish at the bottom of the river where even Poppy would be unable to follow my scent.

Desperately, I resumed my banging. The situation was untenable for long. In the meantime, I decided it might be sensible to conserve my energy, so I stopped hitting the walls and sat down to think. Feeling hungry, I searched my bag and everywhere in the caravan, looking for something to eat. I found a small box of mints at the back of a drawer, the kind where one sweet at a time can be shaken out through a tiny hole in the lid. For some minutes, I was preoccupied with getting all the mints out of the box. At first I ate them one at a time, as they fell out. After a while, I focused on shaking out as many as possible and eating them all together. They did little to assuage my hunger, although they did give me a small energy boost.

Feeling more positive after my meagre snack, I turned my attention back to the door and began to fiddle with the lock again. It didn't seem to have any screws in it, but I wondered whether it might be possible to loosen it and prise it away from the door. It soon became evident that, without any tools, it would be impossible to open the door. There wasn't even a knife or a fork in the kitchen area. Remembering the coke, I retrieved the ring pull from the floor and twisted it off the empty can. Setting to work on trying to loosen the lock, I worked at it for what felt like hours, but succeeded only in making my thumb sore. Giving up, I turned my attention to the windows, but none of them was loose. Kneeling up on the sofa, I worked at the bottom edge of one of them, trying to carve a gap, but it was impossible. My makeshift tool buckled under the pressure, while the window frame was barely scratched.

Clearing a patch of window, I peered out. On the kitchen side, as I had thought, there were only trees and distant houses, too far away to hear me in my sealed prison, however much noise I made. Through the window above the sofa, I struggled to make out the backs of a few caravans which were standing in a row some distance away. My main problem was that I could hear only very faint muffled sounds coming from them. Any noise that I made would be barely audible to the people in those caravans. Whatever subtle sound reached them was likely to be swallowed up in the general noise of their everyday lives.

It was time to take a break from my endeavours and try to think of what to do next. It wasn't exactly going to be a nice cup of tea, but I could drink some rusty boiled water and pretend it was a decent brew. When I turned the tap on the sink, only a few drops of water splashed into the kettle. Then nothing. I felt sick, discovering my meagre supply of water had completely dried up. The first time I had filled the kettle, I must have used the dregs from a water tank that was now empty. Cursing myself for having wasted so much water rinsing it out, I decided to conserve the few drops left in the kettle and ration my drinking. It was a miserable prospect. Other than having no food, and only a thimbleful of rusty water to drink, I had to use what was probably the most disgusting toilet I had ever come across. That alone was enough to spur me on to try and escape.

Having been locked in the caravan for hours, I was frantic with worry about Poppy. My only hope was that Alfie had forgotten about her, in which case she must still be attached to the caravan. Alerting her so she could attract attention seemed to offer my best chance of rescue. I had left her tied up at the back of the caravan, behind the bed, so I clambered across the stinking mattress, kettle in hand, and began banging on the wall, shouting out her name. There was silence. Trying not to cry, I called her again, until my voice grew hoarse with shouting.

I had given up, when I heard a faint bark. Banging and yelling as loudly as possible, even though it strained my throat to shout, I tried to attract her attention. Unsure what she could do to help me, or if it even was Poppy I could hear barking, I continued yelling and making as much noise as possible. There was a chance someone might hear me knocking and calling out, and come to investigate. The possibility of rescue galvanised me and I banged the wall with renewed vigour, beating out what I thought was the morse code for SOS, and shouting for help. Virtually spent, I kept on banging as loudly as I could, and finally I heard voices.

'Move away from the door!' an unfamiliar voice roared.

A few seconds later there was a loud thud, and the whole caravan rocked. A second thud followed, and a third, and finally the door of the caravan flew open, ripped from its rusty hinges. I shrieked for joy as Poppy ran in and jumped up on the bed beside me. I swept her up in my arms and she began to lick my face. Looking round, I saw two stalwart men had forced their way into the caravan. I recognised one of them from the group of fairground workers who had been drinking in The Plough. Behind them, Dana was peering anxiously over their shoulders.

'Are you alright?' she called out. Her voice quivered and she sounded as though she was crying.

Stiffly, I scrambled off the mattress, still holding Poppy tightly in my arms. 'How did you find me?' I asked. 'I guess Poppy had something to do with it?'

Snuggled in my arms, Poppy let out a low growl of contentment as if to reassure me that she had never abandoned me. Dana flung her arms around me, nearly squashing Poppy who squirmed and yapped irritably. Crying and laughing, Dana drew back.

'I'm sorry, Poppy,' she said. 'I'm just so relieved to see Emily.'

Poppy wagged her tail. She understood.

23

Stumbling out of the stinking caravan, I drew in a deep breath of fresh cool night air. A group of showpeople had gathered and were watching me, but there was no sign of Alfie. Sarah was listening to the tall red-haired woman who had warned me to keep away from him the previous evening.

'I knew Alfie was up to no good,' the red-haired woman was saying crossly. 'I told her to steer clear of him.'

In a way, she reminded me of my mother. Despite my irritation I couldn't protest because, underlying her reprimand, she clearly had my interests at heart, so I hung my head as I awkwardly admitted my reason for wanting to see Alfie. A small crowd gathered to listen in silence as I recounted how Dana and her mother had helped me and my friends implement a plan to discover the truth about Paris's death. When I reached the point where Alfie had left me locked in the old caravan, Dana took over.

'Richard and I were waiting for you and the others to come back. Eventually, Hannah called to say that nothing had happened and they hadn't heard anything from Alfie's caravan, where Sarah had installed the camera. So we all thought that was the end of it, and you must have just gone home. Hannah tried to call you but she said you weren't picking up. She was a bit put out, thinking you had gone home and fallen asleep without letting her know where you were. But just as Richard decided to go to bed, we heard Poppy barking outside in the lane. As soon as I opened the door she ran over to me and tried to drag me out of the house.'

She knelt down beside Poppy who had jumped down out of my arms onto the grass, and was wagging her tail. Stroking her head, Dana looked up at me as she continued. 'Seeing Poppy out on the street by herself, we realised something must be wrong. We ran next door to Rosecroft, to check if you were home and Poppy had managed to slip out, but you weren't there. It was obvious Poppy wanted us to follow her. She insisted on leading us in the direction of the fair and we followed, hoping she would find you. Richard didn't want me to come. He was worried it might not be safe for me to be here. He thought we ought to wait for the police, but I didn't want to delay searching for you. I was afraid you might be in danger. Anyway, Poppy led us straight here.' She leaned down to pet Poppy again. 'We heard you banging inside the old caravan, so we called Barry and he agreed to gather together as many of his colleagues as he could, and meet us here. But we couldn't wait for them.' Impatient to rescue me, Dana had run off to fetch a couple of hefty men who worked on the rides.

'We were that surprised to see her,' one of the men said.

'And even more surprised by what she told us,' the other one added.

'They broke the door in and there you were,' Dana said. 'If it hadn't been for Poppy, we might not have found you for days.'

'By which time I might have been dead,' I said. 'There's no water here and the stench is foul.'

Poppy whimpered and came over to me. Putting her head on my feet, she closed her eyes and growled softly.

'That little dog is purring,' one of the men smiled. 'She's like a kitten.'

Poppy raised her head and let out an indignant bark, and we all laughed.

While we had been talking, more of the fairground people had arrived and were listening to Dana.

'The police should be here soon,' I said, looking around. 'Does anyone know where Alfie is?'

My words prompted a buzz of concerned muttering among the assembled fairground workers.

'We'll deal with Alfie ourselves,' one of my rescuers said, clenching his fists. 'We don't need the police here, disrupting our lives and poking their noses in where they're not wanted.'

When I protested that such a serious crime was a matter for the police, he shook his head.

'We're already treated with suspicion wherever we go,' the red-haired woman explained bitterly. 'If anything's stolen when we're in the area, everyone blames us. Imagine what it would do to our reputation, if it gets out that one of us is a murderer.'

'The tabloids will have a field day,' Sarah added.

'Alfie should have thought of that before he killed Paris,' I replied. 'And before he locked me in there.'

'It will be disastrous for us if the police interfere,' one of his friends agreed. 'And we don't even know for sure that he's guilty of anything.'

'He told me he killed Paris,' I pointed out indignantly.

'No disrespect, but we only have your word for that,' one of the men replied. 'You could be making a mistake.'

Lizzie stepped forward. 'She's not making a mistake,' she said in a tremulous voice. 'Alfie told me he killed Paris to get her out of the way so we could be together. I always knew that wasn't why he did it, but I thought no one would believe me if I said anything, and I was scared.' She began to cry. 'He said I knew what would happen to me if I told anyone, and he said I knew he would do it, because he had killed Paris when she defied him.'

'He would have killed me too,' Dana said. 'Emily's right. We have to hand him over to the police.'

'And how is that going to look, if one of us is arrested for murder?' the red-haired woman demanded.

'What kind of justice will Alfie get?' someone else asked.

'What justice did he give Paris?' I countered.

'We don't need outsiders involved in our affairs,' one of the men who had rescued me insisted.

'It's too late for that,' I said. 'Alfie's already involved me, and there's no way I'm going to keep quiet about what he did to me, or what he told me.'

Before long, even Alfie's staunchest supporters agreed he had gone too far for them to try and protect him. In any case, Barry was on his way. He arrived, accompanied by several uniformed policemen, with Hannah, Adam and Toby following them.

'Are you hurt?' Hannah asked, rushing up to me in consternation.

'Where is he?' Barry demanded fiercely.

Before we could continue the conversation, Hannah insisted on taking me back to Rosecroft so I could shower and eat. I was only too happy to agree, because I was starving.

'And you stink,' Hannah added, holding her nose and grimacing.

'You'd stink too if you'd been locked in that foul caravan all evening,' I retorted. 'I can't tell you how disgusting it was.'

Barry accompanied us back to the cottage, where he insisted I bundle my dirty clothes into a carrier bag for him so he could take them away for evidence.

'He didn't actually assault me,' I assured him.

'I still need to take your clothes,' he said.

'Those are my favourite jeans,' I complained, but he was adamant. 'Oh, all right,' I said. 'But they smell foul.'

An hour later, I was clean and sitting in my living room with a plate of scones and a mug of tea on the table.

'These have never tasted so good!' I told Hannah, as I reached for my third scone. 'So, how did you find me?'

'At first we thought Sarah had put the camera in the wrong caravan, because a different girl was in there, being filmed,' Barry replied.

'But Sarah was adamant she had put it in the right place,' Hannah interjected.

'We had to stop filming, and then we called at Alfie's caravan and Mandy told us we were in the right place but he had just gone out. At that point we knew something had gone wrong,' Barry continued.

'We looked for you but you had vanished off the face of the earth,' Hannah picked up the story. 'And when Alfie returned to his caravan, he flatly denied having seen you at all. We assumed you'd never met him and had gone home when you couldn't find him.'

'He was lying!' I protested indignantly. 'He not only saw me, he locked me in without any food and only a cup's worth of rusty water to drink!'

'We know that now,' Barry replied. 'But when we saw him earlier, he swore blind he hadn't seen you.'

'He was obviously drunk and he stank of whisky, not to mention sweat and God knows what other fetid smells, but there was no sign of the whisky bottle Cliff gave you, and we couldn't prove he'd seen you,' Hannah added.

'Now, if you're feeling up to it, I think it's time you made a statement,' Barry said grimly. 'We need to know exactly what happened between you and Alfie in that caravan.'

I nodded. 'I'm up for it all right. The sooner that monster is behind bars, the better. I've no idea what he was planning to do with me, but I dread to think. He threatened to leave me there to rot, as a punishment for my rejecting him.'

'Well, you're safe now, thanks to Poppy,' Hannah said.

'And now it's going to be Alfie's turn to be locked up,' Barry added gravely. 'And not a moment too soon, if you ask me.'

No one argued with him.

24

IT TOOK ME QUITE a while to record everything I could remember, but I was determined not to leave anything out. Typing it on my iPad helped, as I was able to make revisions and additions while writing it. Once I had finished, my dodgy printer refused to work, so I emailed my statement to Barry's phone. He said my physical signature could be added later. The important thing was to write it all down straightaway, before I could forget what had happened.

'I don't think I'm ever going to forget any of this,' I told him, with a grimace.

'You'd be surprised the tricks the mind can play,' he replied. 'It's quite common for people who usually have very good memories to struggle to recall traumatic experiences, or even to embellish them. That's why, the sooner you write it all down the better, while it's still fresh in your mind.'

When it was done, I read my account aloud. Hannah and Adam listened in shocked silence, while Barry sat poker-faced, leaning forward in his chair without reacting, although I was sure he was paying close attention to every word I uttered. There was silence for a few minutes when I finished.

Finally, Barry spoke. 'Did you embrace?'

'Embrace that brute? Are you kidding? No way!' I shuddered.

'Did he touch you? Was there any contact between you? Think carefully. This could be important.'

I shook my head and was surprised when he appeared to be disappointed.

'He hit me in the stomach with a whisky bottle. Does that count? He didn't really hurt me,' I added. 'He just frightened me. It was the bottle Cliff gave me. Alfie downed a good half of it without passing out.'

'You didn't put that in your statement,' Barry said. 'Add it now.'

Too tired to remonstrate, I did as he asked, although it hardly seemed relevant.

'We'll send your clothes off to be tested,' he said when I had finished adding a few sentences about the alcohol, and how Alfie had hit me with the bottle, causing me to bang my hip on the table.

'I've got a massive bruise to prove it,' I added, rubbing my sore hip.

'If he can down half a bottle of whisky without passing out, then I'd say he's got a problem with alcohol,' Adam said. 'Good. He'll find prison even more difficult to cope with.'

Poppy ran to the door, barking, just as the bell rang. Having given her statement to one of Barry's colleagues at the fair, Dana had come to join us.

'They made us all give statements,' she told us, when Hannah had brought her some tea. 'Me and Steve and Mick who broke the door down to reach you. It was really disgusting in there. The toilet!' She shuddered. 'I wouldn't lock a pig in a revolting hole like that. Goodness knows what was growing in that filthy mould. He was probably growing enough lethal bacteria to kill us all. I mean, there's dirty and there's dirty. I know Rosecroft isn't exactly spotless–'

'Well, thank you very much!' I exclaimed. 'What's wrong with Rosecroft?'

'But a bit of dust here and there is nothing,' Dana continued, ignoring my interruption, 'compared to the filth and muck in that caravan. It absolutely stank.'

I nodded, remembering the fetid smell in the abandoned caravan.

'And you were shut in there all evening,' Dana added. 'It's inhuman, what he did to you, positively monstrous. It's a pity his cell isn't going to be as foul as that caravan. Prison's too good for him. He should be kept in a pigsty. They ought to lock him in that revolting caravan and leave him there to rot.'

None of us disagreed with her. Barry left for the police station in Swindon to file his report, together with all the statements.

'Can't you do it online?' Hannah asked him. 'Do you have to go all the way to Swindon?'

Barry explained that he needed to deliver my clothes, along with the statements.

'Is that really necessary?' I asked, irritated, and he nodded. 'When can I get my clothes back?'

'When we've finished with them,' was all he would say.

'You know, sometimes you can be really annoying,' I complained, and he grinned.

'That's more like it,' he said. 'I'm glad to see you've got your feistiness back.'

'I'm not feisty,' I protested, and he laughed. For a second, I was tempted to fling my arms around him.

It was late by the time Barry returned, and we headed back to the fairground encampment. This time Barry led the way, accompanied by three of his colleagues. All four of them were tall and broad, and in uniform. Reassured by their presence, I strode confidently towards the caravans. Barry had arranged to meet Sarah at the edge of the site, and we saw her waving at us before we were close enough to talk. She led us past the outer ring of caravans. Other fairground workers joined us as we made our way to the centre of the camp. Even in the presence of four uniformed officers and a group of fairground people who were walking purposefully with us, I struggled to control a rush of anxiety as we made our way through the warren of vehicles.

Hannah reached out and took my hand and we walked on side by side, with Barry in front of us and Adam behind us. Poppy marched ahead of us without once stopping to sniff the ground, as though she understood that we were embarking on a serious mission. The walk seemed interminable, but at last we stopped by a smart white caravan in the centre of the encampment. A thin red stripe ran around it and painted on the side was the name: Alfie. Each letter was a different colour, and they were framed in gold paint. There was no need for Sarah to tell us that we had arrived. By this time a sizeable crowd of fairground workers had joined us to form a ring around Alfie's caravan. No one made a sound.

Barry broke the silence, striding forward to rap on the door which was opened almost immediately by a blonde girl. She looked very young. Seeing who was calling she drew back, looking alarmed. The girl tried to slam the door shut, but Barry stuck his boot out to prevent it closing. As she turned her head to face him, the light from inside the caravan fell on her and I saw that one of her eyes was bruised above a swollen cheek.

'I see he hasn't wasted any time,' Lizzie hissed, stepping forward out of the crowd. 'What the hell do you think you're doing in there, Mandy?'

The other girl shook her head, looking at Lizzie with a terrified expression.

'Is Alfie in?' Barry asked.

'He's not in,' Mandy stammered. 'He's not here. He's gone out. I don't know where he is. He didn't say when he'll be back.'

'You won't mind us taking a look inside then,' Barry said.

'No, no, you can't come in without a search warrant,' Mandy said, with unexpected pluck.

Without warning, Poppy darted forwards. Distracted by what was happening, I let her lead slip through my fingers. Before anyone could stop her, she leaped over Barry's boot and disappeared into the caravan.

'Poppy,' I called out in alarm. 'Come back. Poppy!'

From inside the caravan, we heard a man yell, followed by a squeal from Poppy.

'Poppy!' I shrieked. 'Poppy!'

'Out of the way,' Barry snapped at the terrified girl hovering in the doorway. She refused to budge.

Two burly showmen ran forward and pushed past her. We heard Alfie shouting and swearing at them to get their hands off him. Yelling that they would be sorry, he threatened to banish them from the fair. A moment later they dragged him out of the caravan, complaining loudly and threatening them for manhandling him. He stopped in astonishment on seeing me, standing outside with my friends and several police officers. Taking in the crowd of familiar faces watching him, he straightened up and his frown vanished.

'Emily,' he greeted me, with a broad grin. 'I wondered when you'd be coming to visit me.' He nodded uneasily at his captors. 'I knew she wouldn't be able to stay away from me for long. Where have you been hiding out?' he asked, turning back to me. 'I looked for you last night but I couldn't find you anywhere. Where were you?'

I shook my head, incensed at his bold lie. Evidently he was preparing to deny the accusation that he had deliberately left me trapped in an abandoned caravan. He was clever enough to concoct a plausible story, claiming I had wandered in there by mistake, looking for him, and had accidentally locked myself in. It might even be possible for DNA evidence of his presence there to be inconclusive. Worried that he was going to get away with his treatment of me, I shook with rage. But the police had more resources at their disposal than he or I realised.

'We know you left Emily locked in an abandoned caravan,' Barry said calmly, stepping forward.

'Lies, all lies,' Alfie answered, appearing equally composed. 'It's no secret that you pigs persecute people like me. I'm the victim here, not her,' he declaimed, raising his voice dramatically and gazing around at the watching fairground community. 'Remember that, all of you. We never trust the police. Anyway,' he continued, turning to glare at Barry, 'you lot are making a big mistake if you think you can browbeat me into making a false confession, when we both know perfectly well you can't prove I was there. The silly cow must have got herself locked in and now she's blaming me so she doesn't have to admit to everyone how stupid she is.' He glared at me. 'You can count yourself lucky I'm not going to sue you for slandering my good name. Let go of me, you idiots,' he said, turning to the two showmen who were still gripping his arms. 'Are you seriously going to believe that girl over me? This is me, Alfie. It's all lies, I'm telling you.'

Barry repeated his accusation.

Alfie glared at him. 'Where's your proof?'

Barry pointed to Alfie's dirty white T-shirt.

'Was he wearing this last night?'

I nodded. 'It could be the same one. It looks similar anyway.'

Barry turned to one of his colleagues. 'Take it off him, and gather up any white T-shirts you can find in there.' He gestured at Alfie's caravan. 'Put them in separate evidence bags.'

'None of that is going to prove anything,' Alfie scoffed. 'You can't prove I went anywhere near her. I never touched her.'

Barry turned back to Alfie. 'You think you're clever don't you? Well, you're right, up to a point. DNA evidence can only prove you were in that caravan. It can't establish *when* you were there. So you're right, DNA can't prove you were there at the same time as Emily.'

With a confident grin, Alfie tried to shrug off his captors. 'Get off me,' he ordered them.

'Not so fast,' Barry said. 'There's no way we are going to release you just yet.'

'You can and you will, right now!' Alfie replied, his voice rising in frustration. 'This is blatant persecution.

You've got nothing on me. You just admitted it yourself. You're going to let me go, right now, or I'll get you for this. You're going to lose your job, pig! And that's all of you,' he added, looking around at the other police officers who were all watching him impassively.

Barry resumed, speaking in the same level tone. 'The problem for you is that forensics are going to analyse samples of fibres they find on Emily's clothes and your clothes, and they'll be able to establish whether any physical contact took place between the two of you. If your sleeves so much as brushed past each other, however briefly, each will have left a contact trace on the other. And now comes the really interesting part. Not only will they be able to prove the contact took place, but they can narrow down, with a fair degree of accuracy, when that contact took place. Even if you and Emily never physically touched, if you lay down on the mattress in that caravan, you will have left traces there. We have witnesses who are prepared to attest to the fact that Emily was in the caravan last night, so as long as you were there too, on the mattress, we'll be able to prove you were there at the same time.' He held up a bag. 'The T-shirt you were wearing last night is going to give us all the proof we need.' He turned to me and smiled. 'Once all the evidence has been gathered and processed, you can have your clothes back, but it may take a while.'

'It'll be worth the wait,' I assured him, returning his smile.

'You ugly cow,' Alfie suddenly shouted at me. 'Whatever made me want to have anything to do with you? I should have finished you off when I had the chance.'

'Like you did to Paris?' I retorted angrily. 'You think

you're clever, but everyone knows you killed Paris. You're far too stupid to get away with it.'

'But I did get away with it,' he replied, his eyes seeming to bulge out of their sockets and his face turning red with rage. 'No one saw me up there on the wheel with her, and I didn't even have to climb down. By the time she hit the ground, the wheel had already carried me halfway down. All I had to do was step off and join the crowd of onlookers—' He broke off and looked around, suddenly remembering where he was and who else was there, listening to him.

'It looks like you got your confession after all,' Hannah murmured to me as the showmen handed Alfie over to the police.

They led him away, protesting vociferously about police brutality and persecution. But his complaints had become halfhearted. For Alfie, the game was over.

We all gathered at the pub that evening, and Cliff stood everyone a round of drinks to celebrate my rescue and the successful outcome of the murder investigation.

'Even though the police had nothing to do with it,' he added.

'It was all down to Poppy,' I said, and everyone cheered.

'And Dana and her friends at the fair,' Richard added.

The usual group of showpeople entered the pub. After a moment's hesitation, Cliff told them it was a drink on the house for everyone that evening.

'Even us?' one of them asked, clearly unsure whether to believe what he was hearing.

'Especially you,' I called out. 'It wasn't your fault Alfie turned out to be a psychopath.'

'Although they were probably shielding him,' Barry

muttered, but I frowned at him and he raised his glass at them in a reluctant gesture of goodwill.

The pub was buzzing that evening. When Dana walked in, I moved my chair over to give her room to sit with us.

'I won't be staying in the village,' she told us. 'I'm leaving in the morning.'

Dismayed by this unexpected news, I asked her whether she had found a job and she nodded. Hannah looked down to pet Poppy, and I couldn't help noticing that she looked pleased.

'This is a bit sudden,' I protested. 'Where are you going?'

'Oh, here and there,' Dana replied. 'I'm going to be helping my mother.'

'Your mother? You mean you're returning to the fair?' I glanced over at the showpeople who were talking and laughing on the other side of the bar.

'It's where I belong,' Dana said. 'It's where I've always belonged, really. I made the best of it, but I never really settled away from my family.'

I thought about all the times I had seen Dana when she was working as a journalist. Back then, she had always struck me as bitter, but I realised now that she had been unhappy. She stood up, bent down to give me a quick peck on the cheek, and lifted Poppy up.

'I'm going to miss you most of all,' she murmured, kissing Poppy's head and holding her close. 'Until next year, little one,' she whispered, and Poppy wagged her tail.

Putting Poppy down, Dana went to sit with the showpeople. Watching her laughing with Sarah and the red-haired woman, I thought how happy she looked.

For me and Poppy, home was a snug cottage in the picturesque village of Ashton Mead; Dana's home was on the road. But our lives had crossed and as she glanced up and smiled at me, I knew we would always be friends.

Acknowledgements

I would like to thank everyone on the team at The Crime and Mystery Club for their continuing support for The Poppy Mystery Tales: Ion, Claire, Demi, Ellie and Lisa. I am really fortunate to be working with such a dedicated and good-natured team of consummate professionals. My thanks also go to Steven for his meticulous proofreading, and to Steve for his lovely cover design incorporating Phillipa's fun and original artwork. I have a sneaking suspicion that they do all the hard work behind the scenes, while I just play with Poppy and indulge my passion for storytelling.

I would like to add my special thanks to all the readers who have contacted me to say how much they are enjoying meeting Poppy in her Mystery Tales. I hope you continue to enjoy reading about Poppy's adventures!

As for the real Poppy, I wish you health and happiness in a long life filled with treats, romping in the grass, and sniffing the breeze.

My final word of thanks goes to Michael, who is my rock in this chaotic universe.

If you enjoyed Poppy Plays Fair, don't miss the other Poppy Mystery Tales!

After losing her job and her boyfriend, Emily is devastated. As she is puzzling over what to do with the rest of her life, she is surprised to learn that her great aunt has died, leaving Emily her cottage in the picturesque Wiltshire village of Ashton Mead. But there is one condition to her inheritance: she finds herself the unwilling owner of a pet. Not knowing what to expect, Emily sets off for the village, hoping to make a new life for herself.

When Emily decides to investigate the mysterious disappearance of a neighbour, she unwittingly puts her own life in danger...

When Emily stumbles on the body of a woman who apparently drowned in the river, the other villagers suspect foul play and are quick to blame Richard, Emily's next-door neighbour and a newcomer to the village. Emily finds it hard to believe her friendly neighbour could be a cold-hearted murderer, and when she meets Richard's attractive son, Adam, her feelings only become more complicated.

Determined to find out the truth behind the death in the village, Emily travels to London to track down the man with whom Richard's wife was having an affair.

Unlike the other residents of Ashton Mead, Silas Strang and his mother have a bad reputation. Rude and aggressive, they terrorise their neighbours and no one stops them. That is until Silas sets his sights on Emily's beloved dog Poppy, which Emily won't stand for. After a public altercation, Silas is mysteriously murdered. To Emily's dismay, the police view her as their number one suspect.

Assisted by her friends, Hannah and Toby, Emily sets out to establish the truth and clear her name... but her enquiries have frightening consequences.

A French patisserie opens in the village of Ashton Mead in time for Christmas. Local residents are pleased but Hannah, owner of the Sunshine Tea Shoppe, feels threatened by the competition.

    When the owner of the patisserie is killed, Hannah is suspected of murdering her business rival. Her friend, Emily, is determined to clear Hannah's name.

Emily seems to be facing an impossible task... until her little dog Poppy makes a surprising discovery.

About the Author

Alongside her popular DI Geraldine Steel detective novels (published by No Exit Press), **LEIGH RUSSELL** is the author of the Poppy Mystery Tales, a cosy crime series set in an idyllic English village. Leigh has an MA in English Literature from the University of Kent. She has been shortlisted for the CWA New Blood Dagger Award, the CWA Dagger in the Library, and the People's Book Prize. Keen to support new writers, Leigh chairs the CWA Debut Dagger Judges, and is a Fellow of the Royal Literary Fund. Leigh lives in London, near her two daughters and granddaughter. One of her daughters has a rescue puppy who inspired the Poppy Mystery Tales.

LEIGHRUSSELL.CO.UK

OLDCASTLE BOOKS

POSSIBLY THE UK'S SMALLEST
INDEPENDENT PUBLISHING GROUP

Oldcastle Books is an independent publishing company formed in 1985 dedicated to providing an eclectic range of titles with a nod to the popular culture of the day.

Imprints include our lists about the film industry, KAMERA BOOKS & CREATIVE ESSENTIALS. We have dabbled in the classics, with PULP! THE CLASSICS, taken a punt on gambling books with HIGH STAKES, provided in-depth overviews with POCKET ESSENTIALS and covered a wide range in the eponymous OLDCASTLE BOOKS list. Most recently we have welcomed two new sister imprints with THE CRIME & MYSTERY CLUB and VERVE, home to great, original, page-turning fiction.

oldcastlebooks.com

| OLDCASTLE BOOKS | CREATIVE ESSENTIALS | THE CRIME & MYSTERY CLUB
| POCKET ESSENTIALS | PULP! THE CLASSICS | VERVE BOOKS
| KAMERA BOOKS | HIGHSTAKES PUBLISHING |